Traces

by

DENISE WEIMER

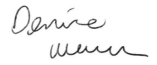

Bling!
Romance
Lighthouse Publishing of the Carolinas

TRACES BY DENISE WEIMER
Bling! is an imprint of LPCBooks
a division of Iron Stream Media
100 Missionary Ridge, Birmingham, AL 35242

ISBN: 978-1-64526-258-9
Copyright © 2020 by Denise Weimer
Cover design by Megan McCullough
Interior design by Karthick Srinivasan

Available in print from your local bookstore, online, or from the publisher at:
ShopLPC.com

For more information on this book and the author visit:
https://deniseweimerbooks.webs.com

Brought to you by the creative team at LPCBooks: Eddie Jones, Shonda Savage, Karen Saari, Jessica Nelson

Library of Congress Cataloging-in-Publication Data
Weimer, Denise.
Traces / Denise Weimer 1st ed.

Printed in the United States of America

PRAISE FOR *TRACES*

Denise Weimer has knocked the ball out of the park on this riveting page-turner. Readers are on the edge of their seats as a reality show becomes the stage for murder and intrigue.

~**Patricia Bradley**
Author of The Logan Point Series
Memphis Cold Case Novels
Natchez Trace Park Ranger Books

Equal parts techno-thriller, reality show, and romance, Weimer's newest book drops you into a fast-paced storyline that could very well take place today. This twisting plot delivers a happily-ever-after and enough suspense for romantics and adventurers alike!

~**Susan L. Tuttle**
Author of *Love You, Truly*

The latest from Denise Weimer is a fast-paced tale of love on the run. A reality television show was just the beginning, but when chased by more than technology ripped from the headlines, who can they trust? *Traces* is romantic suspense at its finest, and you won't want to miss it!

~**Candee Fick**
Author of *Sing a New Song* (The Wardrobe Series)

ACKNOWLEDGMENTS

Special thanks for helping *Traces* reach publication is due to my agent, Linda S. Glaz of Hartline Literary Agency. With diligence and patience, she guided the transformation of this novel from first person to two-viewpoint deep point of view third person, and from a shorter version to a longer version. Then she searched until she located the right publisher and imprint. Thank you, Linda.

Once the story found a home at BLING!, Managing Editor Jessica Nelson and General Editor Karen Saari helped me edit and polish the story until it was ready for print. You both did an amazing job and were a joy to work with.

I also deeply appreciate the efforts of my launch team, who are helping promote my new releases with enthusiasm and generosity. You know who you are. Thank you.

And to my readers, thank you for investing your time and interest reading *Traces*. I hope this story of what "might be" in surveillance technology keeps you anxiously turning the pages.

*Inspired by actual technology used by the U.S. military and adapted
to monitor the 2016 Rio Olympics*

Chapter One

Present-Day Atlanta, Georgia
Mid-April
1:35 p.m.

Kate Carson tapped the toe of her designer pumps and arched a brow at the floor numbers counting ever-so-slowly up in the SurveyCorp elevator. Late. She was late. Well, that's what Helen got for texting about a last-minute meeting while Kate was enjoying sweet-and-sour chicken on the other side of the lake in Piedmont Park—a tardy public relations manager with an orange stain on her blouse.

Glancing down, she attempted to pull her lapel over the blotch, but the collar fell just short of concealing her take-out transgression. Unless she wanted to wear her blazer backwards.

"Yeah, that would make a great impression." Talking to herself was acceptable since she was alone in the elevator.

Thankfully, Kate found overseeing external communications for the nation's foremost surveillance technology developer less challenging than feeding herself.

Who was she meeting, anyway? All Helen O'Ruark told her was that it concerned the project to which she'd devoted ninety percent of her waking hours this last year. The Eye Above Atlanta.

Up to this point, she'd primarily promoted the Stingray-type surveillance technology the company sold to government and law enforcement agencies that captured cell phone information with portable towers. But The Eye took her job to a whole new level. She'd written most of the press promoting the rotating, thirteen-eye camera her company had redesigned from military use, assuring citizens it would provide unprecedented protection against crime when it was

1

installed atop this very skyscraper in two weeks.

Her mother's high school friend—now VP of public relations—could expect favors. But she couldn't expect miracles. One could only traipse a mile in heels so fast.

The doors parted. Before Kate came to work here, a foundering bank had brokered a deal to lease the top fifteen stories of their massive skyscraper to SurveyCorp, offering an elite headquarters for the company's network of development warehouses. Anyone Helen met in the fiftieth-floor boardroom was important.

She furrowed her brow, tucked her chin to check that stain again, and stepped off the elevator—right into a mountain of a man. "Umph."

"Hey!" A deep voice rumbled from the broad, black-clad chest in front of her. "Watch where you're going."

"Sorry."

When she stumbled backward, hands shot up to brace her shoulders. "Are you okay?"

"Yeah." Kate glanced up and clammed up. *G.I. Joe?* From his lash-studded, chocolate-brown eyes to his wide, muscular arms still steadying her, the security guard she'd often seen behind the front desk proved even more handsome inches away. Blatant masculinity always unsettled her, especially when it got close enough that she smelled aftershave. What was he doing up here? She gave a rueful smile. "That's what I get for being in a hurry. Which I always am. You, however, hardly deserve to be head-butted."

He flashed a quick smile. Oh, laugh lines. "It's okay, but you've got …" Grimacing, he pointed to her blouse before taking an awkward swipe at adjusting the earpiece he wore.

"Trust me, I know." Rolling her eyes, Kate gave another tug to her lapel. She edged past him and swept her arm toward the elevator. "Going down?"

"Yes. Thanks." With the customary military stiffness he always displayed behind the front desk, G. I. Joe stepped into the space she'd vacated. He pressed the button for his floor, then his eyes met hers.

A rogue question popped out of her. "What's your name?"

His straight, dark eyebrows shot up. Great. He thought she was coming on to him, but she could hardly explain that it didn't seem politically correct to keep calling him G. I. Joe in her head.

"Alex. Alex Mitchell." He frowned as if parting with the information pained him.

"Kate Carson." As the doors slid shut, she resisted the ridiculous urge to salute. Instead, she pivoted and hurried down the hall. Why had she chatted him up, anyway? To prove she could interact with someone she found intimidating? Must be the MSG.

Bright sunshine slanting through the conference room windows made Kate blink as she opened the door. Poised and professional, her brown hair in a twist, Helen O'Ruark stood, and with her, two men. Both surprises. As he smoothed his tie, Clayton Barnes' aristocratic features relaxed into a warm smile. Kate released her breath. If the man she was dating was here, this meeting must be good.

The other guest, a sandy-haired man in a trendy tie but no sports coat, rushed forward to shake her hand. "Kate, I'm delighted to meet you." He paused, searing her with his gaze.

"Um, it's a pleasure. I'm sorry I'm a bit late." Kate pumped his hand in an attempt to convey enthusiasm.

In response, he squeezed too tight. "That's all right. We put you on the spot. When Helen told me about you, I said I had to meet you today. No delay. I'm Brian Young."

"Good to meet you, Mr. Young."

Helen spoke up. "Kate, Brian produces *Traces*." When Kate gave a slow nod, lips parted as she wracked her brain for meaning, Helen prompted further. "The TV show."

"Oh! Of course." Kate snapped her fingers. Suddenly, Alex Mitchell's presence on the floor made a lot of sense. He'd probably escorted the producer to the conference room. "Where bounty hunters, former marshals, and profilers use technology to track fugitives on a reality show. I didn't miss an episode of the last four seasons. It's my favorite reality show—well, not surprisingly, I guess." As she took the seat Helen indicated, she quirked her smile to one side.

Brian sat across the table but leaned forward. "I'm glad to hear you're a fan … because our next season will be filmed right here in Atlanta."

"Really?" Kate glanced at Clayton with a smile.

His gaze flashing to her sweet-and-sour stain, he smoothed out a frown and nodded. "They're adding a detective from the Atlanta Police Department." Like Alex's, his presence made sense now since he served as press secretary for his father, the mayor. "Our office has pledged full support."

Adjusting her blazer, Kate turned back to Brian. "This is because of The Eye, isn't it?"

The producer tapped his fingers together. "The controversy surrounding its installation makes perfect fodder. Using the camera to surveille the recent Olympics was one thing. Locating it permanently atop Atlanta's tallest skyscraper is another. I mean, let's be honest. Who wouldn't feel a little uneasy at the thought of such a powerful piece of technology linked with the city's existing surveillance systems? It uses infrared technology and can zoom at will. People are scared it will be peeking into their bedrooms." He released a high-pitched chuckle.

Kate stiffened. "Then I hope you're going to tell me how filming Traces here would be to our advantage."

"You know that we expedited the work we were already doing on The Eye after the bombing outside the Fox Theatre." Helen swiveled her chair toward Kate. "We knew we needed to move while public opinion was in our favor. We believe Traces will stir those same emotions."

Kate nodded. This past Christmas, two children and their father attending The Nutcracker ballet had died when a van parked on a side street outside the historic theatre exploded. She would never forget the televised, wailing anguish of the mother, spared from death by a last-minute dash to the restroom.

Brian spread his hands, a big gold ring glinting on the right one. "Obviously, there are areas not covered by the cameras of Operation Shield. Seeing firsthand how The Eye enhances the current system, and how local police use the data to solve crime, should increase public support for law enforcement *and* surveillance technology."

Kate knit her brows and shot a glance at Helen. "Okay. That's great. But why am I here? What do you need me to do?"

Brian grinned. "We need you to be one of the fugitives."

The fugitives? Kate swallowed past the massive obstruction suddenly lodged in her throat. On the show, people went on the run, off the grid, sleeping under bridges and in strangers' homes to evade the trackers. Hitchhiking. Dumpster-diving when their cash ran out. They hardly slept, hardly ate, and didn't wear makeup.

Only her mother knew what she looked like without makeup.

Outside the window, sunshine glinted upon a jetliner descending to Hartsfield-Jackson. Kate wished she were on it, anywhere but here, because Helen was watching her. Which meant she supported this harebrained scheme.

"Why me?" She managed to squeak her question out.

"You're young, pretty, successful. TV material." Brian snatched a pen from his pocket and twirled it. "Watching a hot corporate chick on the run will bump ratings through the roof."

Did that shallow list represent the sum total of her assets? She ran her fingers down a strand of her long, red hair, then folded both hands in her lap.

Shooting Brian a faint frown, Helen flattened a hand on the table and appealed to Kate. "From my perspective, SurveyCorp has a lot at stake. If The Eye Above Atlanta makes a noticeable dent in crime, other cities will get in line for installation. What could provide positive publicity better than a SurveyCorp employee participating in this contest?"

She could get out of this with logic. "Exactly. I have a vested interest in The Eye succeeding. Why would people even buy that I'm trying to win?"

Clayton's hand brushed her sleeve. He spoke softly. "How about a $250,000 down payment on a place of your own, so you can stop writing those exorbitant lease checks?"

"Think about it, Kate." Helen pressed her thin lips together. Did she know Kate had barely made a dent in the credit card debt—and the money she insisted on paying back to her mother—from the wasted months of unemployment and rejected query letters following college, not even two years ago? It was Helen who'd thrown Kate a career lifeline when her Great American Novel turned into her Great American Failure. "SurveyCorp wants you to do this, win or lose."

She was saying this would be good for Kate's job, for advancement. For the success she knew Kate craved. And in her firm statement, was there a bit of threat too? Kate had never taken Helen, a middle-aged, single mom like her own mother, as one to threaten. But neither had she figured her one to alter creation dates on documents.

The morning after the bombing, Helen had a press release waiting. It announced the first action Mayor-Elect Gerald Barnes would take upon assuming office—contracting with SurveyCorp to install The Eye Above Atlanta. Kate wrote press releases. All of them. But Helen had written this one. And so fast that Kate couldn't stop thinking about it. After she sent it out to the news outlets, she'd pulled up the time stamps on the document.

Brian interrupted her introspection. "Five hundred thousand's a lot of prize money, even split two ways."

"Two ways?"

He nodded. "Helen and Clayton are right. You have motivation—money. And your insider knowledge makes you a viable contestant. You'll have a partner, someone with the skills, connections, and competitive nature necessary to provide a strong chance of evading the hunters."

"I've recommended your brother." Clayton smiled at her.

"Since Lance Carson is a veteran officer of the Gwinnett County Sheriff's Office, we'll consider it." Brian stood, snagging a remote that lay at the end of the table. "I have a video that explains everything."

The lights dimmed as Helen clicked the remote for the shades.

Clayton's arm bumped hers as he leaned his blond head close to murmur. "Everyone will be rooting for you. Besides, we all know how much you love a good spy mystery. Now instead of writing one, you get to be *in* one—on TV."

Kate gave a faint nod, but her lunch churned in her stomach. She attempted to focus on the images of traffic and technology that flashed across the wall-mounted monitor. A narrator's deep, compelling voice began.

TRACES. We leave traces everywhere. Our DNA on a door handle. Our face on a surveillance camera. Our virtual trail on a cell phone call. Our physical trail on a license tag reader. Are you bold enough, savvy enough, to evade a team of tracking professionals for twenty days? Can you stay off the grid longer than five other teams to capture the $500,000 cash prize?

Evade The Eye for five days inside Atlanta's Perimeter, relocating at least two times, before expanding the search grid to a one-hundred-mile radius for the remainder of the competition.

Kate glanced at Clayton, and his blue eyes crinkled with a reassuring smile. He seemed to want her to participate for herself, whereas she was less certain of Helen's motivations.

Under the table, he ran the tip of his shoe down Kate's bare leg, reminding her that he wasn't totally safe, either, for different reasons. He'd invited her to spend the upcoming weekend at his family's cabin on Lake Allatoona. There was no doubt he made her blood race. Had since they first met in journalism school, then reconnected at a gala for SurveyCorp stockholders.

Clayton was witty, expressive, melting her with his bold, vulnerable declarations of his feelings, so different from the reserve Kate remembered from her father. Not to mention that everything about him screamed old money and power. The faith instilled in her since her youth encouraged her to wait on a permanent commitment before intimacy. If Clayton might be that man, should she consider setting aside her morals to keep his interest?

The narrator continued, voice intense.

You have two weeks to make your decision, lay any plans, and notify contacts. Once you click the link we send to your cell phone, you will receive instructions to hand over one packed bag and no more than two hundred dollars cash so that all participants have a level playing field. These will be returned to you when you go on the run—which could then happen at any moment. You cannot open a new cell phone account. When you go on the run, Traces *handlers confiscate the registered phone.*

You'll proceed directly to a prearranged location where you will meet your assigned partner. Combine your assets to avoid capture for the twenty-day period, documenting your efforts by wearing a tiny clip-on camera. A production crew with no contact with the hunters will receive the video feed to be cut and aired for each week's show. While on the run, you cannot inform new contacts that you are participating in a TV show.

Good luck. Using leads from your phone, our country's latest technology, and The Eye Above Atlanta ... our team of techno-hunters will find you.

When the video clip ended and Helen raised the blinds, Brian prompted Kate with a grin. "Well? What do you think? This is the chance of a lifetime, Kate Carson." His jiggling leg made his enthusiasm palpable.

Kate wanted only to get out of the room so she could process this crazy turn of events. "I don't know. Can I have a little time?"

Brian stood up. "Yes. You don't have to decide right now." He walked around the long conference table to deliver a slick, black folder. A wave of expensive cologne came with him. "Here are the ground rules of the program along with medical and legal waivers. Look them over. You have two weeks without our surveillance to research and lay plans to go off the grid. You can decline participation at any time by contacting me at the number provided in the folder. We already have a substitute lined up."

Helen interrupted. "Though we much prefer you."

"Right." Brian returned to his seat. "We hope you'll participate. As the video stated, we'll send a link to your cell phone. Within two hours of clicking it, you'll give into our keeping the cash and packed bag. After that, the game could begin at any moment."

"I understand," Kate said, although she wasn't sure she did. This smacked of one of those life-changing moments, an offer she was going to wish had never been made.

2:23 p.m.

Sliding into the elevator with Clayton, Kate clasped her planner in front of her like a shield. He still made her so nervous. She smiled. "We on for dinner?"

Kate half hoped, half feared he'd haul her against him when the doors closed. But that didn't happen, and neither did an answer to her question, because Helen darted inside.

"A little stunned?" She smirked as Kate selected their floor.

"Yes."

"Do you know what you're going to do?"

"I really don't. I still feel like I'm the last person cut out for going on the run."

"Nonsense. You're smart, motivated, and your mother was telling me again when we had lunch last week how you and your reporter friend Amber used to play Nancy Drew as girls. She said you were obsessed."

Kate laughed. "That was a long time ago."

"Don't let her fool you." Clayton nudged her with his elbow while answering Helen. "I can't stand to be around them even now. I think they're talking and signaling in code all the time."

Kate shot a quelling glance in his direction before turning to Helen. "Did you have a nice lunch with Mom?"

She'd warned Mom not to bring up the press release time stamps. Kate had told her mother about the discrepancy the week it happened, about how she'd sat at her desk for half an hour trying to figure out how the accessed stamp bore the date prior, eleven at night, while the created and modified stamps showed that day's date. Someone probably wrote the release right after the bombing, her mother had suggested.

But that fast? And who besides Helen had the authority to do that?

Helen's face softened. "I did. I'm so glad that conference was in Lawrenceville so Bonnie could take a breather from her demanding work to come meet me."

Helen made Bonnie's job sound as important as her own. Feeling Clayton's gaze on her, Kate shifted. He'd never met her mom. She'd never even told him where her mother worked, behind the front desk of the same dental office she'd started at when Kate's dad died. Somehow, she feared he'd look down on her mother, even though he'd attempt to veil any condescension.

The door chimed and parted. Clayton stepped out on the forty-fifth floor with them, presumably to tell Kate goodbye.

But her employer continued, her voice low. "I think the best of your mom, Kate. And the same of you. But I've noticed you've not seemed yourself lately."

Unease clawed its way up her spine. Kate flattened the folder against her chest. "What do you mean?"

"Well, your mom let on you were unhappy that I've been writing some of the bigger releases, especially the one after the bombing." Lines creased by Helen's eyes as she leaned closer to explain in a soothing tone. "You should know, that had nothing to do with my trust in your skill and everything to do with the gravity of the circumstances. As you can imagine, I'm working in close collaboration with the mayor's office."

"Wait." Kate glanced at Clayton. "Did you have something to do with the press release in response to the bombing?"

Clayton gave a slow blink. "As Helen said, we collaborated. You know my father has been a supporter of SurveyCorp a long time. He made a rapid decision when he needed to."

Shaking her head, Kate followed him when he started walking toward their offices. "Writing a press release with SurveyCorp the very day of the bombing was rapid decision-making for sure."

Clayton stopped abruptly, almost causing a passing intern with a stack of files to run into him. "What are you suggesting?"

"Nothing. It was just ready so early, it threw me off." Kate bit the inside of her cheek, as if she could choke off the blush she felt spreading. This was an intensity from him she didn't like. It felt like he could laser the truth out of her brain, see the flash drive in her purse that contained the screen shot she'd taken of the press release's file properties. She'd not even told her mother that she'd made and kept documentation, but as Clayton had observed before, she was a bad liar. Redirection was necessary. Kate pasted on what she hoped was a flirtatious smile. "Clayton?"

"Yes?"

"Why are you heading into the public relations office?"

As soon as Kate said it, she saw her. Kendra Reed. The Mediterranean beauty leaned against the door of her office, her creamy, sleeveless silk blouse leaving little to the imagination and a cheetah-print skirt exposing long, tanned legs.

Why she even had an office in public relations, Kate didn't know. The director of technology information spent most of her time with the technology development VP, consulting on the SurveyCorp surveillance product catalogs she produced. No one in-house ever saw those, and the reps for government agencies and police departments signed a nondisclosure agreement when they received one. But ever since The Eye got the green light and SurveyCorp partnered with the mayor's office, her focused attentions extended to Clayton.

"I have a meeting with Kendra. It might run late. But we have all weekend, right?" Clayton tore his gaze from the expectantly smiling director to offer Kate a conciliatory glance.

"Sure we do." Tamping down any reaction that might betray neediness, she quirked up one corner of her mouth in what she hoped was a relaxed, reassuring gesture.

As Clayton joined Kendra, Helen's voice reminded Kate of her presence. "I expect the article supporting the use of Stingray equipment by outlying police departments before you leave, Kate."

"Of course. That's no problem." Turning away from the welcoming hand Kendra placed on Clayton's arm, she drew a deep breath. Her ability to focus on the task at hand, even in the midst of chaos, was her journalistic strength, one Kate liked to believe would help her if she did go on the run.

"It's a good time to consider a change of pace, Kate."

Helen's words—accompanied by an unaccustomed frigidity in her stare—pierced Kate's bravado and left her wondering what would happen if she failed to agree.

Chapter Two

Late April
4 p.m.

The Eye could see everything that occurred in Atlanta's public spaces, but it couldn't tell Kate what occurred in the human heart. Right now, ripped by suspicion and betrayal, that was the only thing she needed to know.

Her sunglasses concealed her puffy eyes but did little to diminish the afternoon sun beating down on the rooftop of the SurveyCorp building. Seated with the mayor's staff on the other side of the podium, Clayton watched her, handsome features compressed into an expression of concern. Kendra Reed watched her, too, nude stilettos crossed at the ankle under her chair down the row. SurveyCorp had arranged their PR department to the rear of the VPs for the unveiling of The Eye.

Kate tried to focus on Mayor Barnes and the cordoned area behind him where, within minutes, The Eye Above Atlanta would rise through the cement slab and begin its everlasting vigilance against crime. Every consideration to success had been rendered: extensions to the steel roof above, specially channeled run-off, even extra lenses installed on the steel girders that might have created a blind spot for the rotating camera's thirteen lenses.

Barnes' voice boomed through the microphone as he addressed employees, journalists, and VIPs. "Through Operation Shield of the Atlanta Police Department, thousands of public and privately owned security cameras linked together using software designed to identify suspicious behavior. Yet there are places these cameras can't see."

All *she* could see, over and over, was the moment yesterday when Kendra had emerged from Clayton's bedroom at his family's lake house,

13

a twitch of her full lips betraying her triumph.

Ever since Kate had stormed out, Clayton had blown up her phone, calling and texting. "It's not what it looked like, Kate. We need to talk."

Yeah, right.

She'd been so upset she'd done something foolhardy—pulled over on the way home and clicked the link to participate in *Traces*. Her shaking, crying burst of adrenaline had extended to packing her bag with the items she'd purchased with Lance from the camping store earlier that week, even though she'd kept the receipt and warned him she'd probably return them.

Her brother thought the reality TV show idea a lark. He would. He was all about competition and had even offered his portion of any potential winnings to help her pay Mom. Lance knew how much her debt bothered her, despite her mother's insistence that Kate owed nothing. Regardless, he said, their mother could use the money, and Kate could use the escape.

But this morning, on a clearer head, she'd phoned her brother and Brian Young—well, she'd had to leave a message with an assistant—and confessed her mistake. Both had assured her of their understanding and expressed confidence that Brian would understand too.

She needed to face Clayton sooner rather than later. Cut things off with him. Just not until after the press conference. After leaving her purse and phone in the locked drawer in her desk, Kate took the extra step of avoiding her office.

Was he more worried that she'd caught him with Kendra, or that she might have found something when he'd caught her near his computer?

He ought to be worried. About both.

Perspiration beaded under her navy suit despite the brisk wind scouring the fifty-five-story building. She clasped shaking fingers over the small manila envelope in her blazer pocket. She had to get the flash drive it contained to the one person she could trust. Amber Lassiter.

Hemmed in by other journalists, Amber typed on her iPad, her brunette bob obscuring her face. When she glanced up, her gaze fixed on the mayor as his voice and fist pounded out his indignation.

"Every month, criminals prey upon the weak and indigent. Families can't walk through Centennial Olympic Park at night. And the bombing outside the Fox Theatre, a deed which has now been claimed by a radical terrorist group, destroyed the security we thought we'd created."

Framed against a stomach-clenching backdrop of Midtown visible through Plexiglas and steel rails, the tall, sandy-haired politician opened his palms to the press. "Last fall, my election platform called for stronger city security, an increased police force, and getting the homeless, especially vets like myself, off the streets. As many of you know, I've long been a supporter of the surveillance products engineered by SurveyCorp. But The Eye Above Atlanta, derived from military cameras flown over Iraq and Afghanistan, is like nothing before it. Surveillance begins now … with a new era of freedom and safety for Atlanta's citizens."

As the crowd applauded, Mayor Barnes indicated the area behind him. The hum of a powerful engine vibrated the cement floor. Straining for a better view of the emerging machine, the journalists stood. Armed SurveyCorp security guards dressed in black tightened the perimeter.

As she'd hoped, Amber glanced her way with a grin of anticipation. As discreetly as possible, Kate waved the manila envelope. Not discreetly enough. Kendra swiveled her dark head, and Kate fumbled to slide the envelope back into her pocket.

Surrounded by a host of videoing, photo-taking journalists, all intent on the round, black camera extended on its pedestal under the skyscraper's massive spire, Amber furrowed her brow.

SurveyCorp's president, Justin Sandler, took the podium. After allowing only a few questions from the *Atlanta Journal-Constitution* and local TV stations, he thanked the press for attending and informed them that they would be first to exit. G.I Joe—Alex Mitchell, she corrected herself—held open the stair door nearest them.

Kate hurried toward the departing journalists. Amber looked back at her. Raising her hand, Kate made a *C. Confidential …* their

15

childhood code that one of them had a secret to share with the other.

Hand on his com, Alex approached Kate. "SurveyCorp employees are to use the other stairs." Nothing about him indicated that he remembered their elevator meet-cute.

She tried flashing a brief but hopefully dazzling smile. "Hi, again. Kate Carson, remember? I need to talk to my friend a minute." She tried to press past him, but he blocked her.

"My instructions are to ensure the press leaves without mingling."

"Why?"

Behind mirrored sunglasses, Alex's face remained impassive. "Miss Carson, I don't have time to argue with you. I'd rather not have to force you to go."

"Force me?" As Kate looked over his broad shoulder, Amber got swept along in the current of journalists heading to the stairs. Kate let out a growl of frustration and jerked her chin up. "Be assured, I'll report this to the head of security."

Alex Mitchell fake-grinned. "I'll be in my office tomorrow morning to receive your complaint."

What a jerk. She'd been right about him. Fury and embarrassment sent heat rippling over Kate's cheeks. Whirling and stalking away, she headed for the employee stairs, intent on retrieving her phone from her office and setting up a meeting with Amber.

Two men wearing earpieces, dressed in black, barred Kate's path.

She threw her hands up. "What now? I'm an employee, going back to my office."

"No, ma'am. As of this moment, you're on the run. Hand over your cell phone."

"What?" The question came out in a squeak.

"You're on the run. Now!" The ruddy man with the ginger crewcut held out his hand. "Give me your cell phone."

A camera man edged up behind them, and spectators pointed. Kate's mouth dropped open as a solid weight of horror filled her chest. "There must be some mistake. I clicked the link, but I left a message for Mr. Young that I needed to back out."

"We have confirmation from all sources that your participation is a go."

Air whistled in and out of her mouth but failed to reach her lungs. "That can't be right." She glanced back toward the other stairwell, but Alex had disappeared, and a swell of people blocked the remaining guard at the far end of the rooftop. She swallowed. "My phone is in my desk. I'll take you there, but only to make a call and verify what I say."

The man in charge gave a brusque nod.

The handlers escorted Kate to her office and stood by while she unlocked her drawer. Her co-workers, returning to their cubicles and offices and no doubt excited to be part of a pop-culture phenomenon, cheered and recorded videos that would soon go viral. The unwanted attention made her hand shake as she withdrew her phone. She pressed the home button. Nothing. Heart hammering, she held down the restart.

The ginger-haired man peered over her shoulder. When the screen remained black, he grunted. "As I suspected, it's already been deactivated."

"Deactivated? What does that mean? You can't do that." Kate frantically pushed buttons.

His hand snaked out to snatch the device from her, stuffing it in his vest pocket. "Miss Carson, you're not the first person to panic and try to back out. My orders are to escort you to your transportation, and that's what I'm going to do, but you can have someone make a call if you want. If your agreement was canceled, Mr. Young will send someone to extract you."

"Extract me?" Forget *Traces*. She'd landed in the middle of a *Twilight Zone* episode. Why was everyone just standing there, filming her, murmuring to each other? She caught sight of her boss coming to her office door and raised her voice across the workroom. "Helen, I called Mr. Young and left a message to tell him I needed to back out of this, but these men don't seem to believe me."

"If he didn't get the message, perhaps this is meant to be."

"No, it's not meant to be." Kate balled her hands at her sides. "I'm not under arrest. I have rights, and I made my decision. Please, call him. Tell him."

Helen nodded. "If that's what you want, I'll take care of it, Kate, but my guess is that all the teams are already being put in the field." The chief handler's stoic nod confirmed her statement. "You don't want to mess things up for them, too, do you?"

Frankly? At this point? What was one less partnership in the competition? The others would be happy. She just wanted to go home and take three Advil.

"Why don't you go meet your brother, and together you can decide your course of action? Meanwhile, we'll pass your message to Brian."

"Fine. My brother will do whatever I want to do."

"Good luck." Crossing her arms over her chest, Helen nodded to her as the handlers escorted her to the elevator.

Kate didn't like the smug set of her lips.

The handlers didn't break character. The same one who'd spoken before gave instructions once the door closed. "An Uber is waiting for you at the corner. You'll find the backpack you filled and your partner at the gazebo on Lake Clara Meer in Piedmont Park. Surveillance begins at nightfall."

When they reached the ground floor, she strode across the lobby, indignation—and fear—punctuating every high-heeled step. "By nightfall, I'll be back at my apartment eating Chunky Monkey and feeling sorry for other people on reality TV."

Outside, rush hour traffic already clogged the veins of Midtown. The ginger-haired handler opened the back door of a yellow Uber and spoke over her head as she ducked inside. "I hope you read the fine print."

He slammed the door, patted the roof, and stepped away before she formed a reply.

Could he be right? Had she overlooked a retraction clause?

As the silent, Middle Eastern driver made his way northwest, her heart hammered. She tried to crack the window. Locked. The door handle too?

The driver's black eyes lifted to the rearview mirror. As if sensing her panic, he switched on the air conditioning. This was ridiculous. She breathed deeply, willing herself to be calm. Lance might already be waiting for her at the gazebo she knew well from evening strolls.

The Uber dropped her off at the park entrance. Kate darted past trees greening with tender spring toward the lake. Construction signs and tape cordoned off the arched stone bridge, probably a ploy by the TV show to keep the public at bay. A man nearby pressure-washed the cement. She cut him a glance but kept running past the street lamps, across the bridge with black metal railing, onto the white-columned gazebo jutting out into the lake. Ducks quacked under a weeping willow, but the gazebo sat empty except for two backpacks. One belonged to her. Hopefully, the other was Lance's.

Kate knelt next to the unfamiliar bag, unzipped it, and rifled through. Two-way radios, a Coleman first aid kit, Sawyer insect repellent, a compass, a map, a GPS. Those could be his, as could the 75D polyester, V-chamber sleeping bag that inflated with a dozen breaths but packed to three-by-eight inches. Lance had told her he owned one when he'd advised her to purchase the same kind. Nothing like toting around a big bedroll to flag you for surveillance, he'd said. She didn't recognize the clothes. And face paint? Shoe polish? And what was this strange blanket that reminded her of balloons?

"You!"

The indignant male voice caused Kate to drop the crinkly material. Standing at the gazebo entrance, breathing hard, was Alex Mitchell.

She stood. "Why did you follow me here?"

"I didn't follow you. I was told to come here. Why are you going through *my* backpack?"

"Because I expected it to be Lance's backpack."

"Is this some kind of PR stunt?" Alex Mitchell took a knee, stuffing the Mylar back into the knapsack and jerking the zipper shut. He muttered as if to a higher power, "Please, don't tell me she's my partner."

"I'm standing right here!" She jammed a hand on her hip. "And if there's anyone who should be angry, it's me. I was all but guaranteed that if I signed up, my brother, who's an officer with Gwinnett County, would accompany me."

One side of Alex's lips quirked up as those dark brown eyes speared her. "That *but* will get you every time."

"There has to be a way out of this." Kate looked frantically around, as though a smiling game show host would stroll down the path or row up in a gondola, ready to release her from her genie-bottle wish.

The smile disappeared. "You think I would have volunteered for this if I'd realized I'd be babysitting Red the SurveyCorp Poster Girl?" He swept her pencil skirt and pumps with a disdainful glare. "What were they thinking? What a joke."

"Of all the sexist and rudest ..." She bit her tongue. She didn't know this man, and she was alone with him. Would it be wise to provoke him, even if he deserved it? Better to call her brother and get out of here. Only ... her fingers searching her pocket closed not around a phone but around the flash drive.

Lance would have made everything all right. He would have accepted her withdrawal from the show and gone with her to take the drive to Amber. Instead, this arrogant stranger who looked lethal even without his sidearm stood glaring at her. The kind of macho man she'd avoided her whole life. And somehow, she had to make him accept her decision that would leave him partner-less, forcing him to withdraw from a competition that—judging by his current agitation—he'd gone to great lengths to enter.

Chapter Three

Late April
5:30 p.m.

Alex Mitchell regretted his harsh words the moment he'd spoken them, especially when Kate Carson's face twisted in pain. More pain than his statement should have caused, as if her mind wrestled with something else. Not only did she curtail her angry retort, she made a visible effort to calm herself, taking a deep breath that resulted in a sneeze.

"A lot of pollen in the air." He allowed a chuckle to break the tension. "Look, I shouldn't have said what I did. I have this bad habit of joking about something I actually like."

Her eyebrows shot up. "Such as?"

He gestured towards her head. "Such as your hair." *Bombshell* was more the word he'd use. He'd actually been shocked when she told him her name that day on the elevator. He might apologize, but he had no plans to reveal his weakness where her looks were concerned. "So … sorry. I just didn't expect to be teamed with …"

"A woman?"

"Right." Caught looking chauvinistic again, his face heated. His sister would smack him. But it was for her he was doing this crazy thing—her and Mom. "Listen, I need this prize money, and I'm guessing you could use it too."

Kate Carson nodded, but then she hesitated. "I could, but actually …"

Alex's stomach soured. "Actually, what?"

Her face twisted in an apologetic grimace. "I'm not supposed to be here, so maybe you'll get a replacement, anyway."

"What do you mean? Didn't you click the link on your phone to sign up?" His heart rate, still raised from the notice to go on the run, kicked up again. He couldn't afford any delays, much less any cop-outs. He swiped a hand toward her backpack. "You packed a bag."

"I did, but the next morning I changed my mind. I had to leave Brian Young a message, but either his assistant failed to give it to him, or—"

"Or you didn't read the whole contract."

Kate's already fair skin washed out even more. "I can't retract my decision?"

He shook his head. "It was in the fine print. Once you clicked the link …"

"That's what the handler was trying to tell me." Her throat worked. "Helen probably knew too. She probably won't even call Mr. Young."

"Helen?"

"My boss. She told me she would get in touch with him as I was leaving."

"Well, we can't do anything about it now, so why don't we sit down, take a breath, and discuss our next step?" Alex gestured to a nearby bench, but Kate stepped back, her chest rising and falling in rapid movements, her gaze darting again.

"I can do something about it. I can walk out of here and find a phone to use and refuse to participate. What are they going to do? Arrest me? Fine me?"

Evading her gaze, Alex caught his upper lip between his teeth and lifted his black ball cap to run a hand over his hair. She really hadn't read that contract.

Kate's mouth dropped open. "What? There *is* a fine?"

How did a woman who headed up external communications for the nation's top surveillance and security firm overlook such an important detail? Was she that busy? That distracted? "Look, can we just sit down and talk this over?" First of all, he needed to get her out of fight-or-flight mentality. At least, until he could convince her to flee *with* him.

One of her brows furrowed, and she cocked her head. "You wouldn't be letting me believe something false about the contract to keep me in the game, would you? Because I do realize, and not without regret and apology, that if I walk out of here, I leave you high and dry."

Exhaling on a grunt, Alex opened his palms to her. "I'm not that kind of guy."

"So what kind of guy are you?"

"Sit down, and I'll tell you." He eyed the bench.

Reluctantly, Kate dragged her backpack over. Could she even lift the thing? When Alex did likewise, she stared at him as though he might pop out an M-240 and start shooting. He sighed. He definitely had to establish some trust. An unwilling recruit was a dead weight, worse than going it alone—if only that was an option.

They sat down, and he turned to her. "You've seen me around SurveyCorp, right?"

"Of course I have. I see you"—she wiggled her fingers—"standing at the door every day."

Boy, had he seen her, too—struggled not to let his eyes follow her perfect figure in tailored jackets, pencil skirts, and high heels—but letting on that he'd noticed her would be sure to scare her off. And despite himself, his protective instincts were already kicking in. "You know I'm the head security guard."

"So you say, but that's all I know."

"I come from a farm in South Georgia. I have one sister, younger. And the reason I'm in this game ..." He paused, leaning forward with his forearms on his knees, letting his hands dangle. He'd had no intention of opening up this fast to whoever his partner was, certainly not Ginger Barbie.

"Yes?" She prompted him, finally sounding interested. As though her own guard was down.

"My dad is sick."

"Sick, like with cancer?"

"Alzheimer's." Alex chanced a glance at her. Her eyes filled, liquid brown. "He's going to need care soon. My mom can't keep managing him and the farm. The money would help me move them into assisted living."

Kate's lips rounded. "Then you'd move back to the farm?"

Enough sharing time for today. He sat up straight. "Doesn't matter what I'd do. I told you why I need the money, and to get the money, I need a partner."

"I see." The two words sounded contemplative and a little chilly.

Had he been too brusque, offended her? Maybe so, but he had to set some emotional boundaries up front. He couldn't have her digging at him for a month—not with *that* pretty face.

"Look, as soon as the sun sets, they'll know where you are at all times. All Brian would need to do to pull you out would be to contact his team receiving the video feed we agreed to send."

"I suppose that's true."

"So will you come with me, at least for now?" Alex held his breath as he waited for her answer.

Nibbling her rosy lower lip, Kate studied him. "It's just—I can't understand what they were thinking, putting us together."

"Maybe some sort of ploy for the viewers … to see if we fall in love." He was half joking. He even chuckled, but Kate's resulting grimace still punched his pride.

She frowned. "I hadn't thought of that, and of all people, I should have. Well, we won't give them that satisfaction."

"We don't have to quit before we even start either." Impatience clipped his response, causing Kate to draw her arms around herself.

"I don't know you. I signed up because I thought—"

"Because you thought I was your brother. I get it." Alex gripped the edge of the bench until his knuckles whitened. He'd forgotten how much explanation most females required, and the sun was sinking even as his arsenal of persuasion thinned.

The frown deepened into a glower. "So bite me. I have reservations about walking off into the dark night with a strange man."

The way her last sentence trailed off wrapped around his heart and squeezed. Of course she did. Alex hefted a sigh.

"That's understandable, but all contestants were vetted for this show. My background's clean." At least as far as the law was concerned.

"Look, all I can give you is my word of honor that I'll treat you like my own little sister, protect you, and give it everything I've got to win. Trust me, I don't want to answer to your cop brother after this is over. Or your dad."

Kate made a face he didn't understand, so he made a joke. "Just don't make it hard on me, okay?"

Her back straightened at that. "Excuse me? What kind of person do you take me for? I have a boyfriend."

"Right. Mr. Mayor Junior." Unable to keep the cynicism out of his tone at the thought of the swanky politician, Alex continued before she could react. "Can we move on to deciding where we can go for the night?"

Kate cocked her head. "We can discuss it."

He'd take that as a yes. "Let's compare the plans we laid before surveillance. How many contacts did you reach out to within the perimeter?" Given her job, she probably ate, breathed, and slept social connections. Hopefully, she'd prove to be an asset at least in this area.

"About ten."

He nodded. A good number, but worthless if she hadn't worked things right. "Did you go see them in person?"

Kate drew back from the accusation in his question, verifying his suspicions with her response. "I work long hours. But don't worry, I left nothing on my phone or computer. I mailed them all a note."

"A note. Through the postal service?" He raised his brows.

"Yes. Of course through the postal service."

"Are you aware the USPS takes a photo of every piece of mail it processes?"

"What? No!" Kate's face fell.

Alex quelled his disappointment, forcing himself to soften his tone. "It's okay. Most people don't know that about the post office."

She folded her hands in front of her mouth, closing her eyes for a brief second before looking back at him with renewed conviction. "You see, it will be best if the production crew finds me a replacement. Once we get to ... wherever ... tonight, we can contact them and suggest that. I'll share my reasons for stepping out, and you can ask for a fit partner."

Alex tilted his head as a sense of *déjà vu* struck him, taking him back to another woman he hadn't wanted to be paired with. But this humbler side of Kate Carson made him want to keep her. "I doubt they'll go for that, but we'll worry about that later. All this talking is wasting time."

She ruffled immediately, spine stiffening.

Before she could protest again, Alex held out his hand. "I just mean—we need to get going. But where?"

"I do still have someone who can help." Kate tapped her arm with her finger, gaze distant but intense. "My best friend, Amber Lassiter. She's an up-and-coming journalist with the *AJC*. I have something to give her as soon as possible. It's very important."

He shook his head. "They'll be watching her house."

"We worked out a system in advance. I can signal her at the coffee shop we frequent."

"She'll be there tonight?"

"No, not tonight." Kate's shoulders slumped.

"I have some contacts, friends of friends, who live a little southwest of here between Fifth and Seventh. It's within walking distance."

"I guess that's where we'll go, then." Sounding resigned as she chucked her pumps, Kate reached into her backpack and pulled out bright Nikes.

Alex resisted the urge to roll his eyes. He'd do nothing to discourage her from finally mobilizing. In fact, he hefted her backpack and helped her secure the straps around her arms. For an uncertain minute, she tottered, then nodded.

They walked out of the park past children yelling on the playground and events staff setting up for a wedding reception under a huge, white tent. Following Park Drive, he led them south on Monroe, where traffic crawled along streets lined with flowering dogwoods. Breaks in the trees provided glimpses of the BankCorp-SurveyCorp spire, reminding him that tomorrow, if he could convince Kate to stay with him, the paranoia and hurry would set in. A familiar, lethal energy pushed him into march pace.

Kate stumbled to keep up. "You spent time in the military?"

Unable to suppress a surge of pride, Alex tossed a grin at her. "Still shows?"

Her lips parted and eyes rounded. Did his smile surprise her that much? "Uh, yeah. Besides the fact that you're in security. Most guys in that field are either ex-mil or serious wannabes."

He grunted. "The wannabes scare me."

Kate gave a natural, relaxed laugh that weaseled past his defenses. "I get it. Anyone who thinks they become something by putting on the uniform, without earning it through training and discipline, is not only deluded, but possibly dangerous."

His estimation of her went up about five notches. "Exactly."

"Not a possibility with you."

"Come again?"

Kate waved a delicate-looking hand in his direction. "You have this … confidence, but without the swagger, that says you've had experience. Army?"

Good intuition. He nodded, slowing his pace some to accommodate hers. "Military police."

"Did you see combat?"

"Two tours in Afghanistan." If he didn't look at her as he answered, she might not pry further.

"So you're not married?"

Alex sighed. Unfortunately, she deserved some basic information if he expected her to trust him. "No. Just my parents and my little sister, Jill, like I told you. They live near Albany." He glanced at her. "What about you? City girl?"

"Born in Athens. Mom and my older brother, Lance, the one I thought would be my partner, live in Gwinnett now. He just got engaged and also managed to snag a promotion."

"You seem proud of him." Probably best to focus on that rather than ask why she hadn't mentioned her father.

Kate smiled. Yep, she definitely looked relieved. "I am. Lance is my rock."

Businesses bordering Midtown gave way to established yards and mature trees in the residential sandwich between North Avenue and Peachtree Street Northeast. Some of the homes were well-maintained, others not so much. While any of the houses would fetch a pretty penny due to their location, Kate frowned and nibbled her bottom lip as she eyed their surroundings with something akin to distaste. Her shoulders sagged under the weight of her backpack. Probably hadn't had time to prepare for this test of endurance with extra Pilates.

"Almost there," Alex said to encourage her. "Craig owns the gym where I work out. He also works for the postal service."

"That's how you knew about the photographs of letters."

He offered a brief smile. "His wife, Allie, uses the other half of the building the gym is housed in for a dance studio."

"Thanks for telling me." Kate tossed him a grateful smile. Those freckles on her nose … they were cute. "I like to know what's coming."

The meter on Alex's mental partner-estimation scale dipped again. In his experience, you couldn't put a value on adaptability.

As he turned onto the front walkway of a brick two-story, the smell of grilling chicken assailed them with mouth-watering intensity. They mounted a few steps to the wide, creaking boards of a spacious porch.

Kate nodded toward a second door a few feet from the one Alex knocked on. "A duplex."

Allie appeared behind the screen in workout wear, her dark hair in a ponytail. Her eyes lit up, and she pushed open the door.

"Alex, you stranger! Get in here." The brilliant smile Craig's wife bestowed on him made Alex shift his weight and side-eye Kate. "I know you work out with Craig sometimes, but it shouldn't take a reality show to bring you by. What you do for Craig, you do for me, and I want to give back. I'm your friend too."

"'Course you are, and you can help me out now." Alex grinned, but he prayed the couple wouldn't make a big deal of what he'd done to help them in front of Kate. He turned to her, feeding her obvious curiosity with another scrap of background information. "I went to high school with Craig until his family moved to Atlanta."

She widened her eyes, then nodded. "It's nice that you've remained friends."

"The best of friends. Please, come in." Their hostess held the door open for them to pass into the foyer. She smiled at Kate. "I'm Allie. You must be Alex's partner."

"Well … for the moment." Thankfully, she forestalled questions and explanations by extending her hand to Craig's wife. "I'm Kate."

"Kate works with me at SurveyCorp."

Allie giggled, glancing pointedly at Kate's athletic shoes and navy suit ensemble. "But obviously not in security."

Kate responded with an abashed grin. "No. Public relations. Thank you so much for taking us in."

"Oh, I'm excited to be part of this. It will give me something cool to share with my yoga class." Allie smiled over her shoulder, leading them toward the back of the house. She swiveled around with a grimace. "But I'm afraid I have some bad news. My sister is coming in from Alabama tomorrow for a job interview and bringing her three kids with her. Since I didn't know when or if you'd show up, I couldn't tell her no."

"Of course not." As they stopped in the kitchen, Kate smiled her understanding. "I'm actually hoping you can help us contact the producers to get a replacement for me on the show."

"Oh. Alex was already too much for you?" Allie's gaze cut between them, tentative beneath the teasing.

Best to let Kate field that question. Keeping his expression impassive, Alex dropped his pack on the built-in bench their hostess indicated near the deck door and turned to assist Kate, who blinked at him in surprise. Hm. Clayton Barnes didn't spoil her with gentlemanly attention? Maybe Mr. Mayor Junior only acted the part in public.

Or maybe Alex had just given Kate such a bad first impression she imagined he was totally insensitive. He turned away, not liking that possibility so well.

"No, it wasn't that at all. I mean, of course I was reluctant to go off with a stranger."

As Kate launched into her explanation, a movement past another screen door and a haze of smoke caught his attention. In jeans and a T-shirt that showed off his bulging biceps, his buddy Craig stood over a grill, flipping meat. He waved, and Alex waved back.

"Maybe we can use your computer and see if we can find a number to call?" Kate asked as she concluded her spill.

"Sure. Whatever you want to do. My laptop is on, right there." When Allie gestured to the round, reclaimed wood table, Kate wasted no time in sliding into a chair and typing in an address. Their hostess continued speaking as she rummaged in her freezer. "Although I sure would hate for you to miss out on a grand adventure and a grand prize, Kate. Alex will make a formidable competitor. You stand a good chance of winning."

Kate's fingers stilled over the keyboard. He'd shared his reasons for needing the money. What were hers? "Can I ... use your phone?" She offered an apologetic smile.

"Okay." Allie laid a box of brown rice on the counter and crossed the kitchen to slide Kate her cell. "You'll at least stay for dinner, though, right?"

As Kate paused in dialing a number, Alex answered. "I'm taking you up on the offer of a bed, and I hope Kate will, too, if she can't get an answer tonight. But we don't need to eat up your food. I have some MREs in my bag."

Intercepting Kate's skeptical expression, Allie laughed. "Nonsense. There's more at the store. And it's simple and healthy. Marinated, grilled chicken and veggies. And of course, rice." She plunked a sealed plastic bag in the microwave.

Kate smiled at her. "That sounds wonderful. Thank you."

While Kate held the phone to her ear, then pressed a series of numbers for an automated menu, Allie raised on her tip-toes to nab a stack of stoneware plates from her gray-painted cabinets. Alex offered to fill some glasses with ice and water. A few minutes later, Craig came inside with a platter of steaming chicken and glistening fresh vegetables.

"Alex! Hey, dude." Craig slid the plate on the counter before hand-clasping Alex. "Man, it's good to see you. You're here on the run, huh?"

"Yep. Only, I think I might lose my partner before I begin."

"Already scared her off, eh?" Craig cracked a grin toward Kate, who rose and extended her hand when Alex introduced her.

Raising her finger with a muttered apology, she paced to the doorway to leave a message on the phone. Alex took the opportunity to explain the situation to his buddy.

Craig frowned and spoke in a low voice. "What are you gonna do if she can't get a replacement and she still dumps you?"

"In that case, I guess I wouldn't have a choice. I'm just praying it won't come to that."

"But you need that money, bro." Shifting his weight, Craig sighed and rubbed his jaw. "If we had the cash to pay you back—"

"Don't even mention it, man." Darting a glance over his shoulder at Kate, Alex rested a hand on Craig's shoulder and lowered his voice. "The rest of that second signing bonus wasn't doing anyone any good just sitting in my account."

"Yeah, that's when you save it for the future, for when your family needs it. If you had done that, you wouldn't even be in this position now." Craig's face twisted with regret.

"Be in what position?"

Alex swiveled as Kate asked the question from directly behind him. How much had she heard? He turned to face her. "Nothing, just discussing strategy. Any luck with your call?"

He'd successfully diverted her. Her face wreathed in disappointment, and she shook her head. "I couldn't get anyone to answer."

Alex put on a placating smile. "Not surprising, given the time. After dinner, we can try booting up those cameras they gave us."

Nodding, Kate handed Allie her phone, then tugged her blazer down into place. No stain today, just well-defined curves. She addressed Craig and Allie. "I'm so sorry. I hate this mix-up. Can I help with anything?"

A beeping from the microwave accompanied her question.

Allie smiled. "Sure, you can help me set the table." She hurried over to cut open the rice and pour it in a bowl.

Craig grabbed the platter and indicated a spot at the table for Alex. They made small talk while the women laid out the plates, silverware, and glasses. Kate thanked Allie until Allie threatened to take away Kate's plate if she didn't stop. She immediately bit her lip and fell silent.

Alex suppressed a smile. He could appreciate the fact that Kate didn't want to be a burden to anyone … and recognized when it was time to zip it.

Once everyone was seated, Allie and Craig dug right in, while Alex bowed his head for a second to pray. He looked up to find Kate staring at him. She wouldn't be the first to think faith didn't gel with his tough manner. When Alex smiled at her, she took a sip of water and looked away. Was that guilt on her face?

If Allie noticed any discomfort on Kate's part, she didn't pull any punches. Blowing on a forkful of rice, she sat forward and offered a direct if gentle question. "Kate, do you mind me asking why you want to get out of this competition so bad? I mean, you must have had a reason you signed up in the first place."

"I did. Like Craig, I want to help my mom. I have … some debts to settle. But I knew all along I was ill-suited to this type of thing." Kate took another hurried sip of her water.

"What do you mean?"

She gave a nervous laugh. Why did her discomfort make Alex so uncomfortable too? As though a giant hand constricted his heart? "I just … don't do well with the unexpected. I guess I'm kind of a control freak. That's probably why I like working in public relations. You know, even when things go bad, I can guide the outcome, stay on top of it. Not being able to do that—well, it makes me nervous." She poked at her chicken. "And that makes me sound super appealing, right?"

Allie hurried to reassure her. "Oh no, we don't feel like that at all. I think we're all that way to some extent."

"Yeah, but probably not the extent that I am. For a while, I had to take anxiety—" She pressed her lips together and shot a glance Alex's way, her cheeks pink. "Let's just say I don't like people seeing me at my worst, and here I signed up to broadcast everything I'd be bad at to the whole world."

Alex quirked his mouth in a gentle smile. "You care a lot about your mom. I can relate."

"Which is going to make it all the harder for me to let you down." She balled her fist on the table. "You deserve a better partner, anyway. We just have to find a replacement. I never would have clicked that link if I hadn't been so upset."

He drew his brows together and was about to question her about that when Craig broke in. "Let's just say they don't let you opt out, Kate, and for Alex's sake, you stay in. You have several days to kill before you can go outside the 285 perimeter—the interstate around the city. You guys need to make a plan, right?" He rested his forearms on the table.

Alex gave a grim chuckle as he sliced his chicken. "Maybe you can help us with that."

Kate sighed. "If I had to stay in this, I'd need to contact my journalist friend Amber tomorrow. Without fail."

He responded to the questioning gazes of his friends. "Kate has something important to give her."

"Oh, like what?" Allie's brown eyes rounded.

Kate slid a bell pepper off to the side of her plate and speared a squash. "A flash drive with some information about The Eye. A couple of things raised concern for me, and I need her to look into them. But that's all I should say."

"Understood. Wow, this is starting to sound like a real-life techno-thriller." Allie swirled her fork through the air in an expressive circle.

Craig knit his thick brows as he focused on Kate and the problem at hand. "If she's your good friend, how do you propose to contact her without being spotted by the hunters?"

"I told Alex in the park, we worked out a code before this started. Long before we were college roommates and communications majors,

Amber and I grew up playing Nancy Drew and spy club in Athens."

Alex attempted to cover a wince. If she thought this reality show would be anything like adolescent sleuthing, she might be right about her lack of suitability as a partner.

"Go on." Allie seemed more intrigued than put off.

"There's a coffee house near her apartment in Old Fourth Ward called Heavenly Grounds. They keep books on the shelves for customers. There's a second edition of *The Quest of the Missing Map* that we agreed to circle the page number in to represent the date we were to meet there at six p.m. after work. She's to check the book every morning when she picks up lattes for her department."

He couldn't take anymore. "Lattes? This isn't a game of Clue, Kate."

"I know that, *Alex*."

"I'm just saying, do you have any idea how intense this could get?" He clamped his lips together. If he started talking about the quick-changes, evasion of facial recognition software, and pursuits he pictured in the near future, he'd only affirm the fears she'd just expressed. And that would be counterproductive.

"Which is why I'm going to do my best to get you a worthy replacement." Kate's lips wobbled, and she wiped condensation from her water glass.

"I don't want you to do that." Alex's words surprised even himself. The stares from around the table nudged him into explanation. "You need to do this, not just for me, but for you. There's something … empowering … when the right training can turn the weakest, most scared recruit into the best soldier."

"I don't want to be a soldier." Her voice faltered. "I want to go home."

"Which is exactly why you shouldn't."

Allie blinked and sat up straight. "It seems to me, Kate, that you have more reasons to complete this thing than to quit it."

"I mean, we can still try to contact the production crew after supper, but if we can't …" Alex reached out to tap Kate's arm. He hated admitting vulnerability, but he didn't have a plan B. "I need you. And

I think you need this too."

"Maybe you could sleep on it," Craig suggested.

"Yeah." Kate stared at their host. "I could sleep on it." She cleared her throat and continued as though nothing had happened. "If we go to the coffee shop tomorrow morning, I'll circle tomorrow's date, but we'll have to beat her there. They open at six."

Alex redirected his attention to his plate, but his heart raced. Had he just taken a little ground? Too early to celebrate. He didn't know this woman well enough. She might make him a promise and then when he woke up in the morning, she could be gone.

Craig polished off his dinner and sat back from the table. "I can drive you."

"That would be great, man." He offered a nod. "I owe you one."

"Coded messages sound cool and all, but can't you just wait for Amber at Heavenly Grounds?" After voicing her question, Allie ran a finger around the lip of her glass.

Alex folded his napkin. "We can't hang out there half the day. The Eye getting glimpses of us in crowds on and off is one thing. Having a lens fixed on us non-stop, close up, is another."

"And the time she comes varies." Kate placed her fork on her plate. "Sometimes before work, sometimes mid-morning."

He glanced at Kate. "Then best to leave the code as you planned and we can lay low in the parks around Old Fourth Ward until the end of the work day."

The spikes of Allie's messy ponytail waved as she bounced in her seat. "I can help with that. I have all sorts of accessories and makeup from recitals and musical theatre. And of course we have extra workout wear that would look natural at a park."

Alex coughed a laugh. "As natural as athletic clothes can look with our backpacks."

Allie's enthusiasm remained undeterred. "You could take a Frisbee and a basketball too. Let's get this cleaned up, and we can take a look. See, Kate, this is going to be fun."

Kate's sideways glance and muttered response prompted Alex to open their bags while she and Allie loaded the dishwasher and Craig scraped off the grill. He found a package containing tiny lapel cameras which looked like buttons right on top. A card with printed instructions told them how to flip the switch underneath to broadcast a live stream, something they had to do at least three hours each day to remain in the game.

He called Kate over. "Pull your chair around and sit beside me, and we'll send a message."

Tucking her hair back from her face, she did so but left a three-inch gap between their chairs.

"Closer."

Another timid scoot on her part and the gap closed to two inches.

With a grunt, Alex grabbed her chair and dragged it flush with his. At her muffled gasp, he held up the button cam. "Do you see how small this thing is? Now, you need to lean in and get your face right next to mine, so they know we both agree to this replacement plan."

As she followed his instructions, Kate's long red hair flowed over his shoulder, smelling of floral shampoo, and he swallowed hard. Alex held up the device.

"Wait." Her hand came up to stop him from flipping the switch.

"What?" When he turned his face toward hers, they almost bumped noses.

"Uh …" She stiffened and leaned back. "We'll have to tell them where we are if we want them to pick me up."

"Yeah."

"Which negates the whole purpose of using Allie and Craig as contacts and makes you easier to find if you continue the game."

"That's an outcome I'll have to factor into my next step, I guess." His pulse picked up a notch at the realization that not only did she care, but she was still hesitating, her bottom lip caught between her teeth as she frowned at him. Still, as much as he wanted to take advantage of her kindness, he couldn't have her regretting the decision later and blaming him for pressuring her. "We'll trust the producers will work it out so that it's fair. Okay?"

Kate started to nod, but Allie drew closer. "But if they don't ... if they don't respond ..." She stopped a few feet away, a dish towel and a platter in her hand. "Maybe you should trust that too. Hmm?"

Kate remained silent, studying Alex.

Allie clasped the platter against her. "You can trust Alex, Kate. He's a good guy, and he deserves this chance. He wouldn't be in this position—needing money—except for us."

Kate's gaze swung to her earnest face. "What do you mean?"

"Allie—" He tried to cut her off, but Allie answered, anyway.

"I had some health problems a while back, before Craig got the second job at the post office with the good benefits. We fell behind in our payments, and we were about to lose the gym. When Alex found out, even though he was overseas then, he transferred money to the bank. A lot of money. He saved us, Kate."

Alex groaned, uncomfortable with the rising emotion of the scene. "I didn't save you, Allie. I helped you."

"At the expense of your own future."

"That was before Dad got sick." In a decisive gesture, he planted his fist into his other palm. "And I refuse to regret helping my only friend I still have from childhood. He'd do the same for me."

"And it kills him that he can't." Allie bit her lip, and her eyes filled with tears.

"There is no debt." When Alex looped his hand gently around Allie's wrist, she nodded, calming, but Kate stared at him with narrowed, evaluating eyes.

Allie stepped over to the nearby counter, and Kate took a deep breath. "You read the fine print, didn't you?"

"Yes, I did. Several times."

"Tell me what it said."

"Basically, once you clicked the link, you were committed. You can contact the producers for extraction if an emergency arises, but if they determine your reason to be anything less, they can impose a fine."

"How much of a fine?"

Alex glanced at Allie before looking back at Kate. "Up to five thousand dollars."

"Five thousand!" Covering her mouth, Kate sank in her seat on a noisy exhale. "I don't have five thousand dollars."

"That's what they're counting on."

Her hand shook. "Put the camera away."

"Kate, let's talk about this. I wanted you to make this decision based on factors other than money."

"What other factors are there?" She blinked moisture from her eyes as she pushed her chair away from the table. Away from him. "It's why we're in this to begin with."

He couldn't argue.

"I'll show you to the guest room." Her tone comforting, Allie extended her arm.

As she led Kate upstairs, Craig came in from the deck and asked if Alex wanted to watch some baseball.

"Sure, man." Despite the generous meal, his gut felt empty, and he doubted he could focus on any game besides the one he'd signed up for. But what else could he have done except tell Kate the truth?

"You okay?" Craig asked as he clicked on the remote.

"Yeah." Alex lowered himself onto the living room sofa where he would be spending the night and ran a hand over his jaw.

"I feel like I missed something."

The shower turned on overhead.

"Kate just asked me what the fine print in our contracts said. I didn't want to tell her she could end up paying five thousand dollars if she withdraws without just cause."

Craig whistled. "That's harsh." He scanned through the listings until he found the channel he wanted. "So she's staying in?"

"For now, anyway. But this isn't how I wanted it. There's no liability greater than a person forced to participate by threat."

"She seems like a smart girl. She'll realize you could have used the fine to twist her arm from the beginning. But you didn't. You're a good guy, Alex." Kicking his legs up in his recliner, his friend glanced at him. "Eventually, she'll want to stay for you."

Alex made a blowing sound with his lips. Now, that was a fantasy for sure. One he wouldn't dare indulge in. But if Kate was moving forward, he needed to at least think about what they could do tomorrow that would buy them another day. Thankfully, he'd planned ahead for most things. As the commentator droned on, he brought in his bag and fished around in it.

Craig noticed what he pulled out and shook his head. "Oh man. I don't know if that's wise ..."

"What's wise?" Allie stood in the doorway, her arms laden with knit and spandex. Her gaze fell on the box. "Oh." She drew her lower lip into a flat-lined grimace. "You'll need some help with that."

"Thanks, Allie." Alex rose.

"I'll do my best, but no promises. She's still upset. Come on, I'm giving these to Kate."

Alex followed his hostess to their small guest bedroom where Kate rummaged in a toiletries bag atop a bed turned back with fresh-smelling sheets—not for her, but for the expected sister. On top of Allie's gift of clothing, he plopped the box.

Kate's eyes swung to the picture of the relaxed and smiling brunette on the front. "What's this?"

Alex folded his arms over his chest. "If you're staying in this game, we'll both have to pull our weight. Tomorrow morning, every camera on every street corner, in every place of business, will be used to search for us. Your hair is a dead giveaway."

"Oh no." Kate backed away until her calves touched the bed. "No way."

"Your hair is gorgeous, but Alex is right, Kate. It's only temporary color." Allie flipped the box over to show her the wording, but Kate averted her face and extended her palm.

"Absolutely not. No one touches my hair."

Alex knit his brows. "This will work, Kate, but I need you to be flexible."

"Flexible? You don't think I'm flexible?" Kate's strident tone wavered. "I didn't try to contact the producers again. I'm still here

39

with you, aren't I? In a strange place … no offense." She cast a glance at Allie, who offered an understanding shrug. "With no idea what to expect tomorrow."

He was used to giving directions to people who didn't question him, but Allie's concerned frown prompted him to try a placating tone. "Yes. All that is true. And I'm grateful."

"I'll go with you tomorrow to meet Amber, and if no one has contacted us by then, I'll ask her to send us somewhere safe. I'll do my part. But some things cross the line." Kate waved at the offending box. "Changing my hair is one of them. I don't care what the boys said in middle school, I've always considered my hair …"

As her voice trailed off, Kate turned away, but not before Alex glimpsed the tears in her eyes. He dropped his arms to his sides and took a step forward.

Her one beauty? Was that what she was going to say? Guilt stabbed him, and he wanted to tell her he didn't see a single thing about her that *wasn't* beautiful. But he didn't know her well enough yet to say that, and anyway, Allie hurried to comfort her, smoothing a hand down her arm.

"I know it seems like a big deal if you've never colored your hair, but changing your looks for costuming can be fun. Think of it as part of the disguise. Hey, Nancy Drew, right?"

Kate glanced at him. The little-girl look on her face reminded him of the way his sister Jill looked at him when she needed her big brother's shoulder to cry on, and something inside him relaxed.

He backed toward the door, holding his hand up. "It's what I think will give us a chance, Kate, but you're right. The decision is not mine. It's yours."

She swallowed hard and looked back at Allie. "Don't you have a wig or something?"

"Sorry." Allie laughed. "But I do know how to apply hair color. Come on, I'll help you."

"Okay." The agreement wobbled on the edge of petulant and grudging.

As Nancy Drew turned an accusing glare on her perceived villain, Alex beat a silent retreat to the baseball game downstairs.

He shoved down a surge of hopeful anticipation. If he actually wanted to win this thing, better to be thought a villain than to let her turn his brain—and his insides—to mush.

Chapter Four

On the Run Day 1
6:30 a.m.

She was still there in the morning, though Alex hardly recognized the brown-haired fitness princess in booty-busting spandex. Judging by Kate's defeated body language, neither did she. He did his best to express his appreciation to both Kate and to their hosts as they said goodbye.

Residents of the Old Fourth Ward prided themselves on their historic homes and a new seventeen-acre park with a lake, splash pad, outdoor theatre, and skate park. When Kate asked about finishing their breakfast at the complex, Alex expressed the same reservations he'd shared about lingering in Heavenly Grounds. Cameras recorded every angle of trendy places.

He hurried Kate out of the coffee shop as soon as she'd marked *The Quest of the Missing Map*, effectively wiping away the smile her café mocha had put on her face. Or maybe her own reflection in the front door accomplished that.

Alex set the pace down the tree-lined street. "We need to head to a less commercialized area."

"I'm not toting my breakfast for a mile like some bag lady. There's an athletic field across the street, and I'm going over." Her elevated chin told him that even though she'd compromised on her hair, he wasn't calling every shot. As she stepped off the sidewalk, a Smart Car with an Old Fourth Ward sticker swerved around her, beeping its horn.

Alex pulled her back by the elbow. "Wait 'til you have the walk signal!"

She snatched her arm away and spluttered. "Just—let me drink my coffee."

Pick your battles. Alex scanned the periphery before settling next to Kate on a bench. *Five or ten minutes won't be so bad.* He forced himself to gentle his tone as he pointed out the obvious. "You know, you're not going to get lattes every morning. You might even have to skip some meals. Can you do that?"

"Of course I can do that."

"I mean, can you do that without jumping down my throat?"

She released a sigh, gaze still fixed over the lid of her coffee. "I'll try."

When his silence prompted a glance in his direction, he raised a brow.

"Yes."

"Thank you. I appreciate that. Assuming we keep going, I want us to win, and we can only do that if we work as a team." As Kate sprinkled brown sugar over her oatmeal, Alex allowed himself to lean back against the bench and ask the question that had been gnawing at him. "I get that you need money for you and your mom, and that you were upset about something when you signed up, but why? Why this show? There are other ways that might have been easier for you."

Her lips quirked to one side. "Not respectably, and not in one month."

Alex chuckled. "You have a point."

"And a lot of debt." She swirled her spoon through the breakfast cereal and lifted a steaming bite.

$250,000 worth? He fixed a sideways frown on her but chose not to voice the question.

"Let's just say I went through a rough patch in life."

"Fair enough."

Kate said nothing further until she finished her oatmeal, licked the spoon, and pressed the lid back on. "I'd like to quit making lease payments and get a place of my own."

Seemed the less he pushed, the more she shared. Alex nodded. "Makes sense."

"And then there was the fact that my boss put a lot of pressure on me to consider *Traces*. Basically said it was my next career move. I owe her a debt, too—of gratitude. She's the one who offered the job that saved me from my rough patch."

"I see." So Kate was something of a people-pleaser. That compassion could be a weakness if she tried to please the wrong people.

"What about you?" She narrowed her eyes at him. "You really bailed out Craig and Allie in a big way, huh?"

He shrugged. "I couldn't just sit by and watch them lose everything."

"That's admirable. It shows you're loyal. And now you need to help your parents."

"That's about the sum of it."

"Well, at least you're not just trying to add to your gun collection like I first thought."

Alex's jaw dropped. "I call that a stereotype. You got something against soldiers?"

"No. I appreciate your service—although I don't care for the drill sergeant demeanor most military guys have." Kate stuffed her trash in the paper bag. "Wanting to help your parents is a noble aspiration. And you're clearly trained for this competition. But I spent a lot of time researching and convincing the public of the effectiveness of The Eye. As much as I want the money, I don't think we'll make it past the perimeter."

She didn't have to voice her lack of conviction. The way she sipped her coffee—eking it out as long as possible, with one ankle crossed over the other and her arm pulled up on the bench between them, free hand dangling—told him Kate possessed no fight-or-flight tendencies. By contrast, the skin prickled on the back of Alex's neck just lingering in one public place so long. He scanned the bushes, his muscles tensing. "Ready to walk on?"

"If we must." But without asking questions this time, Kate followed him toward a swath of trees.

After waiting for her to deposit her bag in a trash can, he resumed the conversation. "You don't know what skills I bring to the table."

"Enlighten me." Her arched eyebrow and teasing grin offered

further invitation.

"It's all in the preparation. After ten weeks of basic, soldiers who intend to become MPs go to Fort Leonard Wood in Missouri. We get advanced training in enforcing military law, investigating crime, internment, and resettlement. Among other things, we learn warrior skills, reconnaissance, surveillance, base camp defense, evasive driving, protective services, and violence intervention."

She offered an exaggerated wink. "You had me at warrior skills."

Was she making fun of him? His straightforward manner of imparting information, which he considered efficient but others seemed to find dull, had provoked not a few jests since his transition to civilian life. Normally, humor at his expense didn't faze him. But the idea of Kate's condescension chafed like a poison ivy rash.

He pointed across the street. "Let's cross here."

"But we're jaywalking."

Definitely a soldier who hadn't been out in the field, or she'd know survival trumped minor rules. "Yes, but we're not under a camera."

"I wonder how many times we'll say that word in the next three weeks." Kate jogged behind him across the street, steps shuffling a little under the unaccustomed weight of her load.

Alex cracked a smile. "And other words. Disguise. Surveillance. *Run.*" Perhaps joking could soften her own form of training.

"Maybe we should make a game out of it. Like Taboo, you know?"

Thumbs hooked in his backpack straps, Alex cut a look at her as they fell into step on the cracked sidewalk. "That the kind of game you played with Clayton Barnes?"

Her face flushed scarlet. "Obviously, you don't like Clayton ..."

But she must, or she wouldn't work so hard to defend him. Why did he care? "I don't know Clayton."

"That's right, you don't, so let's not talk about him. I was asking about The Eye."

"What about it?"

Leaning forward, Kate gave a little puff as she hefted her backpack up again. "You support it, right? I mean, you work at SurveyCorp like me."

"I work there because they offered me a salary I couldn't refuse. But don't doubt my determination to win. I'm looking at this *Traces* thing like an extension of the job—a contract commitment. And whenever I commit, it's the Warrior Ethos." Alex clamped his mouth shut. Kate would hardly understand. In fact, she'd probably make fun of him again.

"What's that?" When he remained silent, she ribbed him with her elbow. "Oh, come on. What is it?"

He stared straight ahead as he recited the sacred mantra. "'I will always place the mission first. I will never accept defeat. I will never quit. I will never leave a fallen comrade.'"

"I like that last part!"

He chuckled, relieved by the enthusiasm in her voice. "For the record, I am for The Eye."

"Because of its military origin?"

Alex tightened his mouth again before he replied, but she wouldn't stop with the questions until she was satisfied. "Saw too many IEDs take innocent lives in Afghanistan. The technology behind The Eye did save lots of soldiers. Now, it's upgraded and offering safety to a whole city."

Kate's tone turned grim. "As a police officer, my brother agrees, but you might not feel the same if you knew everything." She studied the pavement in front of her with way too much interest.

Alex stopped in front of a sketchy-looking grocery and speared her with his stare. "What do you mean?"

She shifted her backpack again and glanced inside the store through the bars on the windows. "I'd rather not say anything until Amber can investigate. Once I give her the flash drive, it will be out of our hands. Just where I want it."

"If this is something I should know ..."

"There's no 'need to know.' It's unrelated to this reality show—at least, I hope so." With a glance at him, Kate pressed her lips together. "Right now, I want to keep moving, because the way that burly man at the checkout counter is staring at me is giving me the creeps."

With a glare through the window, Alex put out an arm to block the stranger's perusal and urge Kate forward. He wanted to press her, but his limited experience already warned him that could backfire. He settled for something of an apology. "This area's not quite as posh as what you're used to."

"I grew up humble." Kate sounded defensive.

"Not this humble."

"Then why are we going to this park?"

"There's a baseball diamond and tennis courts, and big grassy areas where we can hang out for a stretch of time without looking obvious."

"Fine. I hope you won't have to use those warrior skills. Although ..." Kate narrowed her eyes. "I still half think you're doing this competition to keep them sharp. I guess security guarding would get boring."

"Only people who have never been in a combat zone would say that."

In Central Park, he picked a generic-looking location and suggested it was a good time to turn on their lapel cams while they threw the Frisbee. Kate tired out fast, too fast. Alex didn't know how she'd keep up if she couldn't make it through one morning without a mocha and a nap. They stretched out on benches under a pavilion. Alex watched for movement on the tree line while Kate relaxed in a finger of sunshine that reached under the roof. Cocooned in a blanket from her pack, she soon fell asleep. To his consternation, he found it hard to keep an eye on joggers and pedestrians when he could admire that smooth, beautiful face of hers, sweet and relaxed in slumber.

Finally, Alex's empty stomach reminded him of the lunch Allie had packed in his bag. He tried to rummage quietly, but Kate sat up, rubbed her eyes, and accepted the turkey sandwich he offered.

"Morning, sleeping beauty." When she returned his smile, he indicated they should switch off their transmitters. "We should talk about what we're going to do after you meet with Amber." Alex unwrapped his own sandwich and dove in with appreciation.

"I want to ask her to reach out to a friend for us."

He shook his head. The ... um ... *colorful* nature of his contacts might take Kate off guard, but he'd weighed the risks and placed their success above Kate's comfort. "They'll be watching her closely. I have people on call in Underground, Five Points, and East Atlanta."

Her eyes popped open wide, and her throat worked as she struggled to swallow a bite. "Are you kidding? Underground is known to be the most dangerous part of the city, not to mention riddled with cameras. And who do you know in Five Points and East Atlanta? A bartender and a tattoo shop owner?"

Alex couldn't stop the sly grin that stole over his face. If only she knew how close she was. "Maybe."

"Who do you hang out with?" Kate's voice raised into a squeak.

He slid his jacket sleeve up to reveal his army tattoo. "Vets make for a great network. They can be found in all walks of life." *And trusted more than family.*

Kate shuddered, then took a deep gulp of water. "I am more determined than ever to get help from Amber. You may feel safe in those places, but I don't." She screwed the lid back onto the bottle, fast.

"You're safe with me, Kate."

Her name came out low and raspy, freezing her nervous search for an apple.

"But if you insist on the other option, I do have a backup plan."

Kate looked at him. "What's that?"

"I know a place near Lenox Station where we can hide out a couple of days. It's a long walk from Midtown, but possible. We could follow the Beltline Trail walking path and the elevated MARTA lines to cut some kilometers." He paused. Did she even know what MARTA, Metro Atlanta Rapid Transit Authority, stood for?

She nodded. "I've never ridden the trains or buses, but it's impossible not to see them all over the city."

"Okay, well, there's a train station at Lenox Square we can access to leave the perimeter when it's time. But it would be best to wait a while. I don't know how long the house might be open."

"House? What kind of house?" Kate polished her apple, inspected it, and peeled off the bar code sticker.

"An empty one."

"How do you know it's empty?"

"Sheesh, will you stop with the questions? Reconnaissance training, remember?"

"No, I won't stop with the questions. I'm not one of your soldiers here to take your orders." The rapid blinking of those thick eyelashes was enough to remind him of that. She gestured with her apple. "You did have soldiers under you in Afghanistan, didn't you?"

Alex gave a brief, unwilling nod. Bragging was a sign of character weakness.

"I thought so. Well, I'm not one of them, and I need to digest the full plan before I commit. I need to know how you think we're going to use MARTA and where we'd go after that. Okay?"

He sat for a moment, stewing at Kate's insubordination. She had no idea even his silence was protecting her, preventing unnecessary fears, because she didn't yet know she could trust him. But she was right. She wasn't under his command. They were supposed to be partners, a new concept for him. He'd spent his entire life either answering to or being an authoritarian voice. "I bought two Breeze passes off strangers before the game began. The gold MARTA line terminates at Doraville. I purchased a cheap car with cash but haven't transferred the title to my name yet. It's waiting there."

"Wow. That was a big investment on a gamble." She finally crunched into the fruit, her nonchalant comment and gesture making him tense.

"It's not a gamble. I fully intend on winning. But I can sell the car later to any one of several buddies for what I have in it." He waited, tossing breadcrumbs to a nearby squirrel, while Kate finished her apple.

"I'm impressed." She released a sigh. "Maybe your brawn caused me to underestimate your brain."

Displeasure at her clichéd opinion of him caused Alex's response to come out raspy. "Well, thanks."

A teasing smile played around the corners of her mouth. "Kind of how people assume things about only children, pastors' kids, and redheads."

"You said it, not me." Alex raised his hands. "If you recall, I told you that I liked your red hair."

Tucking her now-brown locks behind her ear, Kate's smirk faded. As he had at Craig and Allie's house, he glimpsed a sadness that was not petulant, but insecure. Did a very different woman lurk beneath the flashy clothes, makeup, and bravado? If so, why?

She sighed. "I'll accept your plan if Amber doesn't have a better one. As long as you agree that I can at least ask her."

"Asking about options is always wise."

He did not, however, agree to agree.

Chapter Five

On the Run Day 1
5:55 p.m.

After lunch, they relocated to Renaissance Park, an area consisting only of paved paths that wound through the woods near some condo complexes. Still, Kate felt safer than in the run-down area near Central. Alex also apparently felt safe enough for them to turn their cameras on again.

As they sat on a bench studying maps they'd packed, flipping off the video feed for any discussion of travel routes and contacts, she grew fidgety. After an hour, she moved to the grass and started doing yoga poses. When she lowered herself to the ground and came up in cobra, Alex's eyebrows disappeared under the brim of his cap.

"Now, *that's* not drawing any attention."

Kate glanced down at her neckline, swiveled to a sitting position, and tugged up Allie's fitted workout shirt. Her face heated.

"Sorry. I'm realizing how bad I am at killing time. In my normal life, I run from one thing to the other with my only down time in traffic or in bed."

He cleared his throat. "You do realize that the better acquainted a fugitive is with topographical details of the vicinity, the greater his or her chances of escape."

Kate giggled. "You sound like a page from the MP training manual." But she went to stand behind him. He jumped when she reached down to turn off his camera. "Is it time to head toward the coffee shop yet?"

With a sigh, he reached for his backpack. "I guess. If we walk *very* slowly."

53

As they approached Heavenly Grounds again, Kate's anticipation rose. She'd tell Amber about the two documents on the drive, one from her work computer and one from Clayton's laptop, then ask for the address of any friend who owed Amber a favor. With any luck, she and Alex would be knocking on the unsuspecting party's door before they finished dinner. And with further luck, if Amber fit the pieces together as fast as her journalistic savvy promised, her whistleblowing could extract Kate from this competition by the end of the week.

No need to share that with Alex, of course.

She ignored a pang of regret. It must be over losing the money, because it couldn't be over bailing on Alex. She hardly knew the man, and by all indications, plenty of conflict lay ahead if they continued this partnership. She would make sure they put in a new partner for him. Although if what Amber uncovered proved serious enough, it could potentially shut down the whole game. She couldn't think about that now. The information on the flash drive was more important even than assisted living for Alex's parents.

They waited at the crosswalk facing the coffee shop until receiving the signal. No jaywalking here. Traffic was too heavy. They'd almost reached the far curb when the sound of screeching tires jerked Alex's head up. A black SUV swerved around the corner, making a right turn with no sign of stopping. Kate hadn't processed what was happening before Alex grabbed her and dove for the sidewalk. He rolled under her to cushion her contact, but her right knee scraped the pavement.

"Ow!" Clutching the burning area, she scrambled away from oncoming traffic. The SUV roared down the street, weaving between lanes. When her gaze flitted to the place she'd stood only moments ago and she saw the black marks on the pavement, a hard shudder shook her.

Alex put a hand under the heavy pack, propelling her up. His urgent voice sounded in her ear as his arm wrapped around her. "We need to run, Kate."

"But she's right there!" Kate flung out her arm to indicate the coffee shop. Her wide-eyed friend watched from the window, likely attracted by the screeching tires and beeping horns.

"We can't take the risk." Alex started toward the side street where the car had first appeared, tugging her along by a strap on her bag. When she pulled away and locked her heels on the pavement, he stopped, letting out a gust of breath. "Look, I don't think that was an accident. If I'm right, at best, our cover is—"

"If you're wrong, and some teen driver cruised through an intersection on his phone, we're running away like idiots and missing the only chance I have to connect with Amber."

"I'd rather be wrong than dead."

"Dead? Don't you mean captured?"

"I meant what I said. Something is wrong, Kate. I can feel it." Alex glanced back over his shoulder, then scanned the street ahead. Did he fear the SUV would circle back around?

Kate bent to check her knee. The material of her leggings was frayed, but no blood showed through. That spandex had been good for something, after all. "You're overreacting."

"Think that if you want. I'll take your poor opinion before I get us eliminated or hurt for some rookie mistake. We're sitting ducks out here."

He broke into a jog, tugging Kate along again. Everything in her pulled her back toward Amber. "Alex, would you chill? This is not Afghanistan!"

"Would *you* shut up and trust my instincts for two seconds?"

Her face heating—meaning it flushed the cherry-red it always did when she got angry or embarrassed, courtesy of her ginger complexion—Kate bit the insides of her cheeks. Because Alex obviously believed them to be in real danger, she'd follow along until he calmed down, but then she'd give him a piece of her mind.

"Edgewood," he mumbled. "Got an idea."

When he grabbed Kate's hand, she jerked back. Physical coercion she wouldn't tolerate. His glance at her intercepted searing vitriol.

"Please, Kate, trust me."

"Then don't manhandle me. Ask me."

Alex twisted his face into a mask of exaggerated patience and swept his arm in a courtly gesture toward the Apex loft building. He spoke with a slow emphasis to match. "Will you please come inside with me? Preferably soon?" He ground the last bit out through clenched teeth.

At the same moment, as a customer opened the door, the most delicious tang of wood smoke and cooking meat funneled to Kate's nose. Her empty stomach rumbled. "Since you chose a barbeque joint for our hideout, all right."

Without a backward glance, she followed two middle-aged men inside. She looked around for a hostess, but Alex kept walking past the bar. Steps faltering with uncertainty, Kate followed. The bartender raised his eyebrows. Alex nodded his head left near the kitchen.

"It's not open this early." The employee spoke over the sounds of the ice he shoveled.

"We just want to see it and use the restroom."

See what? When he received a brusque nod, Alex stopped in front of a bookshelf. Seriously? He wanted reading material in the men's room? Kate frowned at him, but he pulled on the wooden frame, and her mouth fell open as the shelf swung open to the right. She stared slack-jawed into another room where a wooden bar hugged a brick wall.

Alex grinned at her reaction. "You've never heard of the Edgewood Speakeasy?"

Kate shook her head as she trailed him through, and he closed the passage behind them. "Well, hopefully, if anyone's following us, neither have they. We can change clothes here. I'm going to give you some of mine so they'll be baggy, and I have some padding to add underneath." Outside the restrooms, he lowered his bag to the floor and rummaged. "Tie this jacket around your middle, under your clothing. Let it hang down some in the back."

She stared at the items he stuffed into her arms. "Why would any woman want to do that?"

"Because we're going to my closest contact, in Underground."

Kate wanted to sit on the floor and cry. In less than twenty-four hours, she'd gone from sleeping in a stranger's house to sleeping on a park bench, to almost getting run over, to visiting a speakeasy, and now apparently she would be spending the night in the pre-Civil War section of Atlanta sealed off when the 1920s viaduct construction elevated the street level … where most of the city's murders now occurred.

"I'd like to turn myself in. This is not worth it. I'd rather work another four years. What's four years?" The humor she attempted to infuse into her tone must have fallen flat, because Alex reached up to touch her arm.

"You like to know what's coming, right? I'm taking you to a sweet old Chinese man who runs a walk-up restaurant—with a buffet."

"The barbeque right here smells delicious."

"We can't stay in this area. This is one of the fastest ways to alter your appearance. Pull your hair up, and put this ball cap on. We'll hike down Hilliard to Decatur Street. That close to Georgia State, people will take us for students." Alex stood up and zipped his backpack. "Fung Chen should have leftovers at closing time. But we have to hurry."

What was the alternative? The MREs in his bag? Hastened along by that grim possibility, Kate went to change. If there was any possibility the driver of that car had anything to do with the show—not to mention, someone with darker motives—they did need to leave the area.

When she came out of the ladies' room, he leaned against the wall, now wearing a blue Polo shirt, jeans, and a Braves cap. The way his face lit up with approval provided Kate with the miserable assurance that she'd succeeded in becoming a tomboy.

She flicked an eyebrow at him. "For the record, someone who looks like you would not be seen with someone who looks like such a slob as me."

Tapping his chest, he broke into a grin. "You think I look handsome?"

"Preppy. You look preppy."

"Uh-huh." With a smug grin, he swung his backpack over his shoulders. "Let's go."

Kneeling down, Kate jerked on the stubborn zipper of her bag. "First, I need a Powerbar."

"You should save that food until there are no other options." Casting a condescending frown over his shoulder, Alex started toward the bookshelf door.

Kate sighed, struggled to heft her load, and followed. She should be glad Rambo was back. After all, she preferred wit and intellect to brusque masculinity. Alex's teasing, boyish side was more difficult to resist.

Chapter Six

On the Run Day 1
6:45 p.m.

What did the bartender think when two completely different people emerged from the bookshelf? Then again, maybe that kind of thing occurred on a regular basis in such digs.

Kate posed the question that kept niggling at her as they set off south. "Why did you think the car accident wasn't an accident?"

"Instinct. Common sense. The timing was too obvious. Besides, I got a glimpse of the driver, a white male wearing a black hat and sunglasses."

"Sounds like the *Traces* handlers. They must have been following Amber and figured out that we had a meet-up."

"If that were the case, Kate, they would have taken us into custody, not run you off the road."

She didn't want to think that through. "I'm sure they knew what they were doing, probably scaring me to keep things realistic for us and exciting for TV audiences."

Alex cut her a deadpan look. "Seriously?"

"I know good PR when I see it."

"And I know intent to harm when I see it. Someone did not want you to make contact with Amber Lassiter."

She shook her head, still not wanting to believe what she herself had feared, that foul dealings in SurveyCorp or the mayor's office, or both, could run so deep that they tunneled into this show. If Alex was right, were the handlers working for the bad guys, or were the people in that SUV not *Traces* employees at all?

To his credit, Alex remained silent as they traipsed across I-85, allowing her time to process.

Despite her padding, Alex's baggy clothes she wore kept slipping. She continually jerked her pants up. And the shirt smelled like him, spicy and earthy, making her very aware of the stoic man beside her. Her body already protested the previous day of bearing a load, and her stomach rumbled a grumpy rhythm. By the time they neared Peachtree Fountains Plaza, Kate fantasized about Kung Pao chicken, sweet and sour chicken, chicken and broccoli, and General Tso's chicken.

Alex reminded her to keep her head down as they entered the purple double doors across from the Convention and Visitors' Bureau.

The setting sun glinted through the dirty glass of a skylight hung with flags from all the different nations—a once-grand welcome to a mall that now encased mostly deserted boutique fronts and faded, artificial greenery. As they rode the escalator down, Kate's unease rose. Thankfully, a cluster of indie-theatre goers got on behind them, laughing and talking loudly.

On the lower level, shopkeepers for shoe stores and cheap clothing and souvenir vendors closed up for the day, dragging metal gates across front entrances. What if Fung Chen did likewise?

"We should hurry. Where's the food court?"

Glancing at his watch, Alex shook his head. "We need to kill a minute until more stores close." He pretended to look at the snack food on a kiosk in the middle of the mall walkway.

Kate was considering spending some of her cash for a bag of trail mix when her companion dug his elbow into her side. She sidestepped and frowned. "Ever heard of just tapping someone?"

Alex tilted his head. "Police. A man and a woman. They're questioning those people, showing them something on a paper."

Kate's eyes popped open wide. "Our picture?"

"Maybe. The task force could have enlisted their help to find us— or the other fugitive teams. Even if that's not the case, if they run our ID for any reason, we're on the radar. There's a bathroom across the hall. Walk over there, nonchalant. Stay in the ladies' room until nine.

I'll come out at the same time."

"Okay."

Kate forced herself to walk slowly. Just as she cast a parting look at Alex for reassurance, an African American woman with grizzled hair and a flapping gray sweater bumped into Kate as she hurried ahead into the bathroom. She trailed a suitcase on wheels and a swath of unsavory B.O. Coughing, Kate followed, sure she could hear Alex chuckling.

The woman rushed into the handicapped stall and slammed the door. The handle of her suitcase snapped down, followed by a thump. Lips rounding, Kate bent and peered at the dirty floor as first the suitcase then the woman's feet disappeared. Well, by golly. She'd just witnessed a homeless woman securing her place for the night by hiding from authorities.

Did they check the bathrooms on a nightly sweep? Would the female officer come in here? She'd intended to freshen up at the sink, but given the unsettling possibility of pursuit, Kate entered a stall too. This was nuts. She should go tell the officers that she was a contestant on *Traces* but she wanted to turn herself in. She could also relate the suspicious incident in front of the coffee shop.

Yet when steps approached the ladies' room, Kate found herself jumping up on the toilet. The outer door opened. She held her breath, closed her eyes. Tried not to imagine the germs touching her new Nikes. Wondered when the instinct to run had kicked in so strongly that it pushed out all common sense.

Yet … she had a very real chance to win a lot of money *and* advance her career. She could put the memory of the black hole of financial ruin and hopelessness from that year after college far behind her. Never again have to worry about ending up like her mom, living paycheck to paycheck with no real purpose in life. Success meant security. And if Alex was right and whomever was involved with dirty dealings over The Eye was after her, she had to try again to get that flash drive to Amber.

The door closed. She waited.

A moment later, a pair of moccasins touched the floor in the stall next to hers. Gingerly, Kate climbed off the toilet. Sheepishly, she exited her stall.

Gray Sweater stood at the sink, pulling a toothbrush out of the front pouch of her suitcase. With a wizened smile, she nodded as Kate approached. She smiled back. The woman did not ask any questions or belittle Kate's squeamishness as Kate wet and soaped two paper towels to wipe the toilet germs from the bottom of her shoes, even though such a gesture must look terribly diva-like to someone who had to survive every day on the streets.

Kate studied her a moment. "Ma'am? Do you have food? Can I buy you some dinner?"

"No need. I have more than enough." The lady patted a paper bag protruding from her suitcase's lower pouch. "Leftovers from the restaurant buffets. They give them away at the end of the day."

Was Kate's dinner in that bag as well? She could've pinched herself at the thought, it was so disgustingly selfish. "All right, if you're sure." Kate checked her watch. Nine p.m. She washed her hands, smiled again at the homeless lady, and pressed a twenty into her hand. "For tomorrow."

The crinkles around the woman's sad, dark-brown eyes drew up as she smiled. "Thank you."

What had happened to her? Kate wanted to take her home, but that would mean leaving the game, a game the woman would probably find ridiculous, if not outrageous and wasteful. Suddenly, shame she couldn't explain propelled her from the restroom.

Alex waited for her, instantly noticing her somber expression. "What's wrong?"

"Nothing."

"Not buying that, but come on. They're gone."

They found the food court deserted. The gate, under a glowing orange sign that read "Golden Sun Chinese," had been pulled closed but not yet latched, and the lights behind the counter were still on. Alex rattled the metal bars. "Fung Chen! Fung Chen, it's me, Alex!"

A small Asian man with gray streaks in his black hair appeared from the rear of the food stand, his almond eyes wide. "Alex! Is it time? The TV show started?"

"Yesterday. We just had a close call in Old Fourth Ward, and we could use your help."

"Of course. I am happy to help my most loyal customer." As Fung Chen pushed his gate wider, he followed Alex's glance up to a security camera on a nearby post. "Oh, don't worry. That one has not worked for several days. Could be the grease I smeared on it, knowing you'd be coming."

Kate gasped at the twinkle in the older man's eyes. "You disabled an APD camera? Isn't that a felony?"

"Only if what he did is permanent." Alex winked at her. Then he said to their host, "This is my partner, Kate."

Fung Chen offered a firm handshake before he pulled the gate closed behind them. "Nice to meet you, Kate."

"Thank you for helping us."

"Come. Come. You're in luck. I have lots of food left over today."

In the kitchen, several steel basins held the varieties of stir fry she'd hoped for. Apparently, Gray Sweater had gotten her dinner from the other restaurants today. Fung Chen set out paper plates and took their drink orders.

"You don't have to wait on us." Alex tried to snag the cups his friend pulled from the top of a tall stack. "I know you need to get home to your family."

"It's no problem. Set your things down in the office." After sliding the cups under the soda fountain, he pointed to a door off the kitchen. "Private bath too."

Kate followed Alex into a small room occupied by a cluttered desk with a five-gallon fish tank, a wooden swivel chair, and a faded yellow sofa. A TV was mounted on one wall, while another door led to a half bath.

Peeking in at the dirty pedestal sink, she swallowed. "This is where we're spending the night?"

"'Fraid so." Alex dropped his heavy pack at the end of the sofa.

"But don't worry. I'll take the floor."

Kate took a minute to divest of her padding in the bathroom. When they went back out into the kitchen, Fung Chen was heaping servings of everything on their plates. "Eat. Eat up! But remember, you stay out of kitchen after this. Police make patrols at night, and you can see kitchen from food court. Be ready to go at ten a.m. My employee knows you may be here, but you must go before the customers come."

Alex nodded. "We understand. And I promise, I'll pay you back for this, Fung Chen."

"Your friendship pays me back." Running detergent and water in the steel basins, Fung Chen grinned. "Besides, after you win, I tell everybody how I helped you, and business will boom. I will have the money to open my own restaurant near the Olympic Park where everyone can see it!"

They laughed, but the undercurrent of wistfulness in the man's voice tugged at Kate's conscience. Her year of failure haunted and drove her, but in the last fifteen minutes she'd encountered two people plagued by far more life challenges than she'd dreamed of. Yet both smiled and acted gracious. How many other stories of broken and unfulfilled dreams did the people of Underground represent?

Grateful for the large Styrofoam cup foaming with ice and Diet Coke, Kate took a long drink, then refilled it under the tap. Fung Chen finished his clean-up before telling them good night. With a wink, the restaurant owner circled the counter and locked the gate. As Kate watched Fung Chen walk away, her breath started coming fast.

For the second time that night, Alex stared at her and asked, "What's wrong?"

"He ... locked us in. Like a prison. We can't get out."

"It's only temporary."

"I'm claustrophobic. Really claustrophobic." All she needed was to show Alex further weakness, but she couldn't control her response. "One time when I was a little girl, my dad had taken his fishing boat out of the shed to clean it up. I climbed into a storage compartment and fell asleep in there. When I woke up, he'd locked me in."

"Oh wow. How long before someone found you?"

"Thankfully, our neighbor came out to water her flowers and heard me screaming."

"A bad feeling, being stuck in a small space." Alex turned her away from the gate, steering her back into the kitchen. He handed over her plate. "They cured us of that pretty quick in basic training."

"What did they do?" Although she wasn't sure she wanted to know.

"Put us in a box we couldn't even straighten our legs in and nailed the lid on, then left us there for four hours ... which seemed like four days."

"It sounds like torture."

He lifted his shoulder. "A necessary part of captivity preparedness. You learn what to focus on, which for you right now is that plate of food." Swiping both their drinks and placing them on the desk, Alex came back with his own plate and closed the door to the kitchen.

Trying to ignore the fact that he'd just created an even smaller cell, one that his broad shoulders and looming height dominated, Kate sorted the onions and peppers to one side of her plate. Her frayed nerves appreciated the fact that Alex didn't try to talk while they ate, and though he turned the TV on, he kept the volume low. The normalcy of a baseball commentator's voice and the familiar tang of sweet and sour chicken slowed her racing brain to a normal pace.

As her hunger was satisfied, Kate began to consider her longing for a shower and the lack thereof. But she could get reasonably fresh using the soap and washcloth in her bag. She shifted her weight forward on the stained sofa.

Before she could get up, Alex glanced over. "Tomorrow morning, we'll start out for Lenox. You should rest up. It will be a long walk."

"I can't leave the area until I assure Amber we're okay and give her the drive. Maybe we can go by her house, and I can leave it on her porch."

"As I have said at least twice already, whoever was in that SUV will be watching her residence."

When Kate started to argue, Alex flipped off the TV and turned to her. "I think it's time you tell me exactly what's on that flash drive."

She sighed. "I maintain that the SUV incident was staged for theatrical purposes. We did sign medical releases."

He shook his head. "Our paperwork stated that no physical force would be used in our pursuit." When Kate pressed her lips together, he continued. "You want me to keep walking into danger, whether from handlers or assassins, I need to know."

She took a slurp of Diet Coke, then plunked her cup on the end table. "Fine. I'll give you the nutshell version. There are two files on the drive that I want her to investigate. The first one is a screenshot from my phone, taken the day after the bombing, of the file properties from the news release." She explained how Helen had the release waiting when she arrived that morning and how the oddity of that caused her to check the time stamps. "The created and modified dates and times were set to early that morning, but the accessed date and time was from eleven the night prior. The night of the bombing."

Alex nodded. "Some software programs allow you to change the time and date a file is created and modified. You can even change the time and date accessed, but if someone goes back in to view the properties, the accessed date reverts back to the true timeframe. Most people don't know that." He responded to her quizzical look by holding his hands open. "What? I had friends in all branches of the military. It's amazing what you learn."

"That's exactly what I suspected about the accessed time." Kate puffed out a breath. "But if someone sent the file to Helen, who? And if she accessed it within an hour of the bombing, how early was the press release written? Minutes after the bombing? Or … days before?"

"Those are questions with serious implications. Maybe someone higher up in the company who was really on the ball? President Sandler?"

"I thought of that. I also considered that Clayton may have drafted the release with his father—or Kendra Reed. She's the director of information technology who writes the descriptions for our product catalogs, even the top secret stuff."

"I know who Kendra Reed is." Alex's deadpan tone told her he held some reservations about the swanky beauty. Kate found more satisfaction in that than she ought to.

"Naturally, Helen and Kendra have been working hand-in-glove with the mayor's office on publicity about The Eye." A tinge of bitterness colored her statement. "But if the release was really written minutes after the bombing, why alter the times to look like the file had been created the next day?"

"Hmm. Either to avoid the appearance of guilt, or because there *was* guilt." Alex rubbed a thumb over his chin, producing a slight rasping sound. "In the park, what was it you said about the mayor's office?"

Remembering that day at the lake, Kate grew still. How could she tell about the second document without exposing the personal pain and embarrassment that lingered under the surface? "I had access to Clayton's laptop one day. I was ... looking for something." Actually, evidence of romantic correspondence after Kate heard him talking on his cell phone from his back deck. She could still mentally replay the suggestive murmurs and fragments of phrases that had roused her sixth sense.

Alex nodded, prompting her to continue.

"I found a list of 'potential threat groups.' People in those groups will be targeted by The Eye to have their information recorded in a classified database."

"What kind of groups? What kind of information?"

"Any information The Eye can collect, to add to whatever the city already has on file."

He sat up straight. "You're talking about full-on spying. Are these radical terrorist groups?"

Kate bit her lip. "Not just them. I didn't have time to read the full report at first. Clayton almost caught me on his computer. I barely had time to copy it onto my flash drive before he found me in his office. I ... made up some excuse about what I was looking for."

"Did he buy it?"

"For the moment."

Kate wasn't proud of the fact that she'd employed some feminine wiles to divert Clayton. When she'd avoided his attempt to get her into the bedroom, Clayton accused her of holding out on him because she believed him to be like her father. Her unfaithful father. Kate's defenses had flared, and so had a full-blown fight. She'd grabbed her bags and driven south toward Atlanta, but she'd pulled off at the first exit for a good cry. She'd wiped her eyes and inserted the flash drive into her laptop right there in the car.

"So the groups on the list, they weren't standard terrorists?" Alex leaned forward, forearms on his thighs, hands dangling.

Kate blinked, coming back to the present. "Not all of them. In addition to Hamas and Al Qaeda, there were other Muslim groups. Neo-Nazis. Groups I had to look up like Kamane, Army of God, Sri Ramsene, and then the real surprises."

"Such as?"

"Orthodox Jews, conservative and evangelical Christians—both Catholic and Protestant —and disgruntled military vets." With this last, she met Alex's eyes. They darkened another shade.

"Does Clayton realize you know about this?"

"After I read the list, I turned the car around and went back to see him, to demand an explanation. Maybe that wasn't so smart, but I had to know. I'd just asked him what he knew about this database when I realized someone else was there." *Kendra.* Kate swallowed, hoping Alex pictured the office setting she tried to imply.

"Did he let it go?"

"He demanded to know if I'd been on his computer. He did seem … defensive." Though Kendra walking out of the bedroom looking like a feline with catnip could've had something to do with that.

Alex shifted, frowned. "What did you say?"

"I left without answering." Kate looked away, into the past. She had fled again, more like it, after choking out through her tears, "Is that all you can say to me now?"

Overwhelmed by Clayton's betrayal, Kate hadn't processed the ramifications of the database yet. She finished in a steadier voice. "On the way home, I pressed the link on my cell phone to join *Traces*, and the next day, the hunt began."

"So he knows," Alex said in a monotone.

"He knows I discovered something."

"And the screenshot of the time stamps?"

As weariness from the long day caught up with her, Kate shook her head. "No one knows I took it. Can we be done now?"

Alex sat forward. Much farther and he'd fall off the couch. "Did you ask questions at work?"

Running her fingers up into her hair, Kate massaged her temples.

His eyes narrowed. "You did. You stuck your nose into something, maybe more than one thing you weren't supposed to know about, and now somebody wants to scare you … or silence you."

Irritated—and if she admitted it, frightened—by the dire tone of Alex's pronouncement, Kate jerked open her backpack and started feeling around for her toiletries. She just wanted sleep. "My boss may have known the timing of the press release confused me, but that's it. No conspiracy theory. It's ridiculous to think any of them would want to harm me. Helen is my mother's childhood friend—the one who gave me the job at SurveyCorp—and Clayton, well, Clayton has feelings for me. So stop trying to make them into criminals who hire assassins." Finding her washcloth, she stood.

Alex's gaze remained fixed on her with unsettling directness. "Kate, what are your instincts telling you? In a situation where something seems suspicious, it probably is. Think this through to the worst-case scenario. If someone at SurveyCorp knew that bomb was going to explode, it means they were probably in on it, counting on the backlash to greenlight the installation of The Eye. Which would make that person or persons very dangerous."

Kate walked all of the four steps to the bathroom before turning. "I get that you're trained to detect danger, Alex, and that's a huge asset for this game, but if I'm going to continue, I can't accept that anyone would take this far enough to infiltrate a reality show to try to stop me.

So let's just concentrate on winning, okay?"

Not waiting for him to reply, she squeezed herself into the tiny room and shut the door. The muddy-haired woman staring back at her from the mirror startled her. After a couple days in the sun, her freckles popped out, and she couldn't rely on her normal arsenal of cosmetics to disguise them. Ugh.

As she turned her gaze toward the water from the faucet warming up, Kate realized she'd forgotten the T-shirt and PJ pants she intended to wear to sleep. With a sigh, she flung the door back open—and discovered an empty office.

Panic made her heart thud. "Alex? Alex!" Had he decided she was too uncooperative and picked the lock on the gate, abandoning her in this underground hole?

A weary sigh and a voice answered from outside the office. "Here."

She cracked the door open to find him stretched out on the floor—which looked so cold and drafty, she shuddered. "What are you doing out there? Fung Chen said we shouldn't be in the kitchen."

"Well, I'm not sleeping mere inches from *you*."

Kate stood there in silence, stunned by the realization that he did find her annoying and demanding. She was accustomed to employing wit and charm to persuade people, especially men. Yet this man's stoic demeanor stood in stark contrast to Clayton's unedited admiration.

Finally, Alex responded to her lingering presence. "Look, I didn't mean that to be insulting. I'm trying to be chivalrous, if you can't tell the difference. No one's going to see me here on the ground. Enjoy the privacy, Kate, and get some sleep."

Kate appreciated that. She did. He was making good on his promise to treat her like a little sister, ensuring that she felt safe. But it was the hurt mingling with her sense of security and relief that puzzled her as she shut the door.

Chapter Seven

On the Run Day 2

Alex stood over Kate and wondered if he'd given up the sofa for nothing. Judging from the amount of sighing and shifting he'd heard through the door overnight, the princess hadn't slept well. Now she nestled far down in her sleeping bag, as if to escape the forty years of contaminants on the sofa. He hated to wake her.

It would be so much easier if he could do this thing alone.

Alex placed a folded shirt and pants next to her head, and she stirred. "Try these today."

Rubbing her eyes, Kate attempted to retreat from his perusal. Did she really feel that insecure without makeup and fancy clothes? Her fresh-faced beauty reminded him of the girl from the farm down the road, the one two years older than he whom he'd had a crush on growing up.

She moaned. "Why can't I wear my own clothes?"

"We're going to a homeless shelter up the street for breakfast. You need to blend in."

"Doubtless the bags under my eyes and my tousled hair qualify."

Alex chuckled, surprised again by Kate's dry humor. Not many people made him laugh.

Kate blinked as she sat up, getting a good look at him. "What did you do to your hair? And … your face? You must be some kind of makeup artist!"

"Easy tricks with talcum powder and a little shading in the creases of the eyes with gray eyeliner." Adding a ball cap over his silver-streaked hair, Alex tugged a longer strand from the front between his brows, then offered an exaggerated wink. "If you want, I'll give you a makeover

71

later too."

As anticipated, his unexpected humor lowered her defenses. Kate laughed. "I guess I should be thankful you haven't insisted on aging me already."

"Not today, but add the padding again."

Her brows lowering, Kate clutched the clothes to her chest.

"You'll need it for the cameras if we track down your friend in Midtown."

At that incentive, Kate nodded.

He tilted his head as he studied her. "You got some real dark base makeup with you?"

She blew out a disgusted breath. "I have foundation with sunscreen that matches my skin tone. Why?"

"You can use some of mine." After digging in his bag, Alex tossed her a small bottle of taupe liquid. "Apply it around your eyes and cheekbones. It can help fool facial recognition software, which relies heavily on eyebrow to nose ratios. Don't you know this from your exposure to surveillance technology?"

"I helped promote it, not develop it, and I certainly did not learn how to evade it."

"All it takes is a little research. Didn't you say you researched The Eye?"

"Maybe my mind isn't as devious—" Kate bit her lip, cutting off whatever she'd been about to say.

He might need her, but there were moments Alex still found it hard to restrain his exasperation that he'd been teamed with a partner who had relied on the postal service to establish contacts. "Sorry. I need to let it go. We've got to hurry if we want breakfast."

"Okay." Kate lowered her gaze. "I need fifteen minutes."

Her conciliation tugged at his chest, and he smiled. "I'm beginning to learn what motivates you."

Half an hour later, with both of them looking as though they'd smeared bad tanning lotion on their cheekbones, Fung Chen's nephew let them out into an echoing food court. Shopkeepers opening their stores cast them wary glances after taking in their backpacks and worn clothing. In the military, Alex had learned to deflect scorn, but Kate visibly wilted under the reversal of roles.

Minutes later, she moaned at the line that curved outside the shelter onto a busy street corner. He'd bet the people huddling in the cool spring sunshine were the variety that she'd always hurried past with averted eyes. He was just hoping none of them remembered him.

As they filed into line, a woman with a small shopping cart bumped Kate's thigh and said, "Excuse *you*."

Alex took Kate's arm as she stepped back, pulling her to his side. "We didn't mean to cut you off, ma'am." He held out his other hand to indicate that she should go ahead.

The woman raised her dimpled chin and pushed her cart forward.

In a tone that showed indignation at the woman's attitude, Kate muttered, "I think we got here at the same time."

Alex gave a warning shake of his head. He recognized a worthy foe when he saw one. When Kate opened her mouth again, he reached down to squeeze her hand. Clearly startled, Kate pinched her lips together. She ducked her head and pulled his coat she was wearing tight around her as a cool breath of early morning, spring wind licked the alley. Suddenly, she stiffened.

"What?" Alex asked, immediately scanning the street.

Kate pulled a wallet-sized photo out of the coat pocket. Her face relaxed into a smile as she held it up. "This your mom and sister?"

He didn't need to assess the likeness to know it showed Jill with her pert little upturned nose and Mom with her salt-and-pepper hair, beaming at her daughter during Jill's senior photo shoot. He snatched the picture and tucked it in his shirt pocket. "Yeah. Forgot I'd stuck that in there yesterday."

"To remind you why you're doing this." Kate tilted her head, studying him. "Are you blushing?"

"Windy out here."

"That is *not* windburn." She nudged him with her elbow. "Why would you be embarrassed? It's sweet."

73

"I don't know too many soldiers, or ex-soldiers, who tote around photos of their mom."

"Well, I know one now. And I'm glad. It helps me picture them too. Jill is cute, and you look like your mom."

When Kate slid her hand onto his arm and squeezed, Alex thought his face might go up in flames. But if the photo helped her personalize his quest, his humiliation might be worth it.

As they drew closer to the door, the scent of fresh bread and coffee wafted out. They'd finally reached the entrance. An African American man standing behind a steel buffet looked up. Not surprisingly—as Alex towered over everyone else—he made eye contact.

"Alex! Aren't you on the wrong side of this counter?"

Too far back to explain, thanks to the stringy-haired woman who dawdled at least two of the lengths of her grocery cart behind the next person in line, Alex grinned and waved. The exchange attracted the attention of a group of grizzled men in army surplus. They, too, turned and waved.

"How do they know you?" Kate whispered.

Alex answered in a low voice. "I volunteer here sometimes. That's Thomas behind the counter, and the vets all served terms in Kandahar."

"Fung Chen, the tattoos, now the homeless shelter. So what do you do, spend all your free time doing errands of mercy in the seedy parts of Atlanta?" The disbelieving question came out a little too loud.

Cart Lady turned and assessed Kate through rheumy, narrowed eyes. "And who are you, the queen of Buckhead? Come to think of it, I've never seen you around here before."

While Kate froze with lips parted, Alex reached for a tray and addressed both the woman and Thomas. "She's with me. We're kind of upside down right now and could use a hot meal."

"Humph." The woman's gaze descended to the new Nikes on Kate's feet, at odds with the old clothing she wore.

As Alex's cosmetically aged countenance came into view, Thomas' eyebrows almost touched his hair net. "No kidding?"

"No kidding."

"No questions, man. I got your back." Thomas plopped a scoop of oatmeal into a plastic dish and extended it to Alex.

As Kate reached for her serving, Cart Lady pulled at a bit of padding that peeked above Kate's belt. "What's that? What tricks are you up to, girlie?"

"Nothing." Going red in the face, Kate leapt back from her questing fingers. "Would you please stop touching me and let me get through this line?"

The woman crunched her already crinkled face into a sneer and raised her rusty voice to mimic Kate in a demeaning falsetto. "'Please stop touching me!'"

Thomas leaned over the metal frame of the counter. "Now, Maude, leave them alone."

Alex angled his body to block the homeless lady, allowing Kate to duck her head and reach for a cup of juice. Women could be as determined as insurgents when it came to guarding their territory. So could he. Right now, Kate was his territory.

Sean, one of the vets he knew, beckoned to them from the coffee station. "Hey, Alex, come join us."

"Sure thing!" He tugged Kate along with him. Better to explain his suspicious appearance to friends than to Maude.

That explanation was demanded sooner rather than later, as the youngest man in the group, stirring his coffee, guffawed at Alex. "Dude, what happened to your hair?"

The edge of Maude's cart came into view. Her voice rose above the din, accusing and quarrelsome. "Who are you people, and what are you up to?"

As heads turned, an elderly man stood from one of the long tables on the other side of the hall. "Maude, you need some help with your coffee?"

"What about *my* coffee?" Kate whispered to Alex.

"You willing to tangle with Maude to get it?"

She tilted her head in careful consideration. "Maybe."

He laughed. "Sit down. I'll go back for it." He gave a pointed glance at the button cam attached to his T-shirt she wore. "We wouldn't want her to notice *that.*"

Kate groaned. "Ugh, I can just imagine how that little episode would get spun ... with me, not Maude, as the butt of the joke."

Was he imagining things, or did a tiny light glow on the electronic device? Alex's stomach bottomed out. "Uh, Kate, is that on?"

"What?" Sliding her tray onto an empty table nearby, she twisted the camera up. "Oh no! It is." She slid the button and looked back at him with her face drained of color. "It wasn't when we left Underground, I swear. I must have turned it on by accident outside, when I pulled my—*your*—coat tighter around me. But they can probably guess our location by the serving line."

It took everything in him not to ditch the tray and drag Kate down the street. Instead, he forced himself to talk to her, to give her the chance to weigh in on their options. "Let's think about it a minute. The coat covered it up until just now, right?"

"Right. At least, I think so." She examined the way the layers of her clothing hung, then nodded as if satisfied.

Sean beckoned them over. "Alex, are you coming?"

"Yeah." He waved, then handed Kate her tray. "It should be fine."

He ignored the hollow sensation in his gut as he led her to the table where the three men in faded green and camo gathered. They nodded as Alex introduced Kate. He'd spent many a Saturday morning chatting with the guys after serving their breakfast, sharing past missions and current life struggles. He found the homeless vets far easier to relate to than civilians.

Sean and Tanner were middle-aged, their skin as leathered as if they'd spent the last year in some Middle Eastern desert, but Carver was only a little older than Kate. His boyish face under a buzz cut and slighter build made him more approachable. With a shy smile, Kate slid her tray onto the table next to his. Alex suppressed a chuckle when she wrinkled her nose. The men smelled as though they'd just finished playing a game of basketball.

When Alex returned with their coffee, Kate was asking them, "So

… you've all been in the military?"

"Yeah." Carver looked up from his tray to offer her a grin. "All of us part of Operation Enduring Freedom like Alex. Me in 2014, Sean and Tanner among the first to roll out in 2009. These guys were career soldiers." Admiration tinged his tone and the glance he sent the older men.

"But not you?"

Carver took a sip of coffee and made a face. "Nah. Couldn't handle it. I got PTSD real bad. My best friend Matt got blowed up by a roadside bomb, a lot like Alex's friend, but Matt only lost both his legs."

At the word *only*, Kate turned to Alex with brows raised. He stirred brown sugar into his oatmeal until she gave up and murmured to Carver, "I'm sorry to hear that."

"You still going to counseling at Veteran Affairs, Carver?" Alex asked.

"Yeah, man."

"Good. Keep it up."

Sean extended his hand on the table. He still wore his wedding ring, even though he'd previously shared with the group that his wife had divorced him over a year ago. "Alex, I applied for that job in the shipping department at SurveyCorp you set up for me. Looks real hopeful."

"Glad to hear it." Alex reached across to grasp Sean's forearm. "I'm proud of y'all. Keep going in the direction you are, and you won't be on the street for long."

Holding her spoon above her oatmeal, Kate surveyed Alex with rounded eyes. "I guess I'm not the only poster child for SurveyCorp."

Alex didn't respond, just smeared grape jelly on his toast. Growing up, his dad had always quoted the Bible passage about not letting your left hand know what your right hand was doing. He'd taken it to heart.

"The way I see it, Mayor Barnes has done more for this city in two months than the last guy did in two years." Sean tore a greasy piece of bacon with his teeth while Tanner nodded his head.

Alex and Kate exchanged a somber glance.

Sean frowned. "What? What's up with you guys, anyway? Why do you look like extras for a bad Soviet spy movie? I'd ask if you're in some kind of trouble, but I know better where Alex is concerned."

Alex wiped his hands on his napkin, then planted his elbows on the table. "Suffice it to say that someone is after us. We're not sure who, but they could be dangerous. And we need to evade surveillance. We can leave Atlanta in a few days. We need to lay low until then."

"You're evading The Eye?" When they nodded in response to Tanner's question, he spewed a laugh with specks of coffee from between yellowed teeth. Inconspicuously, Kate slid back in her chair. "Good luck! Don't take this wrong, but you're gonna fail. And if you were anybody else, I'd say I hope you do. Nobody wants to see safer streets than those who live on 'em."

"We all do." Kate thumbed the lip of her coffee cup. "But not everything may be as it appears."

Sean narrowed his eyes, faded hazel under bushy brows. "Something going on at SurveyCorp I should know about?"

"Maybe." Alex responded to Kate's questioning look with a brief nod. They could trust these guys. But after their close call, he felt better if they put the button cams away. He detached his and held out his hand for Kate's.

She gave it to him, and he slid both into his shirt pocket. Before he could elaborate, Kate turned to the ragged trio. "I can't let you vets believe Mayor Barnes has your best interests at heart when he's got you on a list to surveille as a potential threat group."

"What?" Sean growled the question.

Alex blinked in surprise at Kate's directness. Of course, while she'd expressed disbelief that someone might be after her because of the flash drive and uncertainty over the involvement of her co-workers, she'd never questioned the evidence she'd found about the surveillance database. He could only hope the concerns he'd expressed had cemented her convictions about the rest.

She clenched her hand into a fist on the table. "I work at SurveyCorp, too, and I learned that the mayor plans to keep a database of people considered homeland threats. Military veterans that they'd consider unhappy with the government are among those under his microscope."

Shoving his food aside, Tanner leaned forward. "That's outrageous! Completely opposite of what he said to get elected. Do you have proof?"

Kate nodded. "I don't know how far along plans are, but yes." She swallowed, checking herself from going into further detail. "We're trying to get the proof to my journalist friend so she can investigate."

Carver looked at Alex, shaking his head. "Man, you're in deep ..." He added a few descriptive words. "This is dangerous stuff."

"You have no idea. When Kate tried to contact her friend yesterday, I barely saved her from being run off the road."

"I thought it was a stunt," Kate said to the men, "but Alex went all G.I. Joe on me. I have to admit, I'm not liking the cloak and dagger stuff as much as I thought I would when I was a kid. I miss my own bed—and real coffee." She took a sip, wrinkled her nose, then met Alex's eyes. "I've been thinking since our talk, if you really believe the incident yesterday was intentional, maybe we should find Amber at lunch, then tell these *Traces* people we're through."

"What *Traces* people?" Carver jerked his head back. "Isn't that a TV show?"

Alex ignored him, narrowing his eyes at Kate. "Back to quitting already? We're partners. Fifty-fifty, remember? And personally, I'd like a chance at that $500,000."

"Well, you can have all of it."

He scoffed. "As if they'd let me go on without you."

"They'll find a—"

"You can quit talking about a replacement. If they were going to do that, it would've already happened." He leaned close to her and hissed into her ear. "And what do you think SurveyCorp is going to do when they find out you cast suspicion on them as well as the mayor's office? Offer you a promotion?"

"I ... hadn't thought of it that way." Swilling the coffee in the bottom of her cup, Kate looked sick. "I can live without the prize money, but I can't lose my job."

"You worried about getting fired? You'd be lucky if they didn't frame you."

Tanner nudged Alex's arm. "Uh, guys, I hate to interrupt your little discussion, but are those men in black across the room the ones you're running from?"

Their heads swiveled in unison. Two of the familiar-looking SWAT crew loomed over an indignantly talking Maude. She pointed in their direction. Dread rushed over Alex in a cold flood of adrenaline.

"Back door." Alex lunged into motion while Carver slid Kate's pack over her shoulders.

They darted down a dark, narrow hallway, past a kitchen and storage room. Commotion broke out in the dining hall behind them. Only at the exit did Alex realize Sean followed them.

"What are you doing?"

Sean shooed him on. "You helped me. Now let me help you."

As they dashed into the blinding sunlight, something *whooshed* by Alex's head.

"Shots fired!" Sean pushed Kate, who'd frozen in place, her eyes round with disbelief. "Go, go, go."

She stumbled and stopped again, her head whipping back and forth. "Go where?"

Long-dormant flight instincts kicked in, tunneling Alex's vision to an escape route, a yellow cab parked nearby. "The taxi!"

He jerked Kate forward by the hand, and she stumbled into the car face first with her pack on top of her. He and Sean piled in on either side. "Drive," he shouted at the startled, middle-aged Italian driver, who dangled a half-eaten breakfast sandwich from his mouth as he gaped at them in the rearview mirror.

"Somebody got a hit on you? Get outta my car!"

The *ping* of a bullet contacting metal and Alex and Sean's bellowed commands convinced the driver to swerve into traffic, tires screeching.

The Italian released a string of curses. "Who are you people?"

"Ones who will pay—well!" Alex slid out of his pack.

Kate knelt with her head buried in the seat, struggling for breath.

Alex placed a hand on her arm. "It's okay." When she didn't respond, he rubbed her shoulder gently as he whispered to Sean. "Do you have someone who can help us? I need to get to Lenox where we can regroup, but not in this car."

"Yeah, I have a friend I can call. You got a burner phone?"

Kate raised her head long enough to gasp out a response. "In my pack."

Alex unzipped her bag and handed Sean the phone, then helped her out of the straps and back onto the seat. Without thinking, he curled his arm around her and turned her face onto his shoulder. "Breathe. You're shaking like a leaf."

To his surprise, she didn't resist, but started mumbling a prayer into his shirt while Sean murmured on the phone. Alex asked against her ear, "You still think they're just trying to scare us?"

Kate turned her face up to him. "It could have been an air gun."

He shook his head. "I'd say a .243 with a silencer."

The phone still held to his ear, Sean broke into their conversation. "Yeah. From the top of that four-story building across the street."

Kate's voice wavered, sounding dangerously close to tears. "How did they find us? Is this my fault ... the button cam?"

"Could be. But could also be Underground footage where we entered the food court last night and didn't exit until morning. Maybe The Eye caught us on the street." But enough was enough. They needed to tell the authorities what had just occurred. Releasing her, Alex reached in his shirt pocket to turn on his button cam.

"No!" Kate shoved his hand down. "What are you doing?"

"Sending a SOS."

"What if someone receiving the video feed is compromised?"

He froze. She could be right. But he wasn't ready to tap out, so he offered justification. "They already know we're in this taxi."

"Alex, no."

Ignoring Kate's plea, he hardened his jaw and turned on the mic. He bent down so that his face filled the screen. "Someone just fired shots at us at the homeless shelter in Eastside. Send APD officers to apprehend active shooter."

"Stop it! You're crazy." Kate shook her head as he provided the address. Then she covered her mouth as the driver jerked into a turn lane at a traffic light. "I'm going to be sick."

"Put your head forward." Alex's hand guided her neck until it rested level with her knees.

"Turn it off, turn it off."

Alex shifted, putting the camera away. "Fine, it's off." He angled his body toward Kate, lowering his voice to a whisper. "What do you think about giving the flash drive to Sean? He could go straight to Amber if I give him money for the taxi."

She turned alarmed eyes on him. "A homeless man? Even if you trust him, which obviously you do, once I let that drive go, there's no telling what could happen. If I can't put it directly into Amber's hand myself, I'm only giving it to my brother."

"You have a point." He sighed, scratching his jaw. "Sean's status could throw up road blocks, and they'll have captured him on surveillance. I don't want to put him in danger. Best to give it to someone with the authority to protect it."

Concluding his call, Sean handed Kate's phone back. "Maximo will meet you at the Church of the Holy Trinity off North Avenue. I used to do construction work for him before I tore my shoulder. He's a good guy. He'll drive you anywhere you want to go."

"That's near Midtown Place Shopping Center." Alex leaned up to tap the driver. "You hear? Drop us off at Holy Trinity, then I'll pay you to continue on to Midtown Place. Lose yourself in the traffic before picking someone else up."

A large gold ring glinted as the Italian held up a beefy hand. "Whatever you say, buddy. The quicker I get you outta my car, the better." When he turned around to add an emphatic statement through the metal grate separating them, Alex got a potent whiff of sausage. "And I best get no trouble from the law for this."

Alex bristled. "You won't. I'm a security guard, a former MP. I don't get on the wrong side of the law."

"Sure you are. I get people being shot at every day in my taxi."

"You can drop me at the shopping center," Sean said. "I'll get another cab from there."

When the driver pulled up in front of a church with a domed steeple and elaborate stained glass windows, Alex inspected the shaded parking lot and cluster of buildings before cracking open his door. "Good. Offices are separate. You sure the church will be open?"

"Maximo said it always is."

Alex peeled several bills into the driver's hand, then insisted his friend take several more.

Sean folded them and put them into his pocket, his weathered face further creasing in concern. "Alex, I know you know best, but seems to me it's time to call the police." He sat forward to maintain eye contact as Alex helped Kate out of the taxi. "Explain to them everything that's happened."

She swayed, bracing herself against the roof. "No kidding. We should call them now."

"I have a plan." Alex leaned in to shake Sean's hand. "Kate's brother is with the police. I'm going to take her to him."

As expected, mention of Kate's brother seemed to fortify her, buying Alex a little time. Too much rode on his success in this stupid reality show.

They entered Holy Trinity by a side door leading into a long hallway flanked by classrooms. Halfway to the sanctuary, they found a bathroom. Over the sink, Alex splashed water on his face and drank deeply, his mind rushing ahead. He hoped Maximo drove fast. Whoever had fired at them was probably tracing that taxi cab right now.

Chapter Eight

On the Run Day 2
3:55 p.m.

The white-and-green Gonzales construction truck dropped them off on a shaded side street in front of a small brick ranch mostly hidden behind overgrown shrubs and mature trees. A *for lease* sign barely topped the scraggly grass.

Alex gestured up a cracked concrete driveway. "Let's go."

Clutching the paper bag containing the drive-thru dinner Maximo had provided, Kate followed Alex to a back deck that had long ago lost its coat of stain. "How did you know about this place?" She leaned against the brick beside the door, watching him jimmy the lock.

"Last week, I called up a real estate agent in this area and asked to see the most private and modest places for lease."

Kate gave a grudging grunt of appreciation. "I have to admit, I never would've thought of that."

"I picked several out as possibilities, but for obvious reasons, this one was my favorite. Aha!" He gave a cry of triumph as the door squeaked open and a musty smell wafted out.

"Yes, obvious." Wrinkling her nose, Kate peered into a kitchen with oak cabinets, dated appliances, and green Formica countertops. "Were you counting on the eighties theme and the general air of abandonment to keep anyone from moving in?"

Alex grinned. "That and the ridiculous price tag. I told the agent I didn't mind a higher cost just to get in the area."

"Unfortunately, that's true of a lot of people. This is a perfect fixer upper." Kate stepped inside and tried a light switch. To her surprise, the fluorescent strip above them flickered on, while a table and chairs sat in the adjacent dining area. "Utilities are working. And it's furnished."

After firmly closing the blinds, Alex dropped his pack by the door. "Partially. The last tenants moved out first of the month. Someone could tour the house at any time, so we have to keep our ears open, but we should be safe here a couple of days."

"Days? I thought we were going to my brother. The sooner the better." As Alex strode through a living room furnished with plaid couch and TV and down a dark, Berber-carpeted hallway, Kate followed, still toting her load. A sick feeling blossomed in her stomach. This place was too quiet, too remote.

In a bathroom sporting a floral border atop navy-and-burgundy striped wallpaper and a blue, marbleized-style Formica countertop that coordinated with the one in the kitchen, Alex knelt and lifted out the front of a small storage access in the wall.

Kate watched from the doorway. "What are you doing?"

"*Yes!*" Glancing up with an intense gleam in his eyes, Alex displayed a small black duffel bag. "Took this out of my briefcase during the tour, hoping no one would find it. We've got extra food and supplies in here that will give us another week. And this ..." Unzipping the bag, he removed a handgun from a green hip holster and rifled around, presumably checking for ammo. "Getting my Beretta 9mm back in hand gives me a lot more peace of mind."

Taking a step back, Kate swallowed. The appearance of a firearm only made her think of all the ways a confrontation with the people pursuing them could go wrong. And could she really trust Alex to protect her?

The muscles in his broad back flexed as he replaced the storage access door. Yes, all the people she'd met thus far held him in high esteem, and his actions seemed to support their good opinion. But what *didn't* she know? Just like with her dad, just like with Clayton, men always seemed to have a flip side. Maybe Alex was far more dangerous than Carver from the homeless shelter, shattered by PTSD. What if this game had become some kind of military mission because of him? What if the SWAT guys were not after her, but Alex? "We're not Bonnie and Clyde. Maybe you're enjoying this, but for me, this isn't fun anymore. I want to leave tonight for Gwinnett."

Dragging the duffel to the counter, Alex stood up. "You need rest. You almost passed out this morning. And my plan to get to your brother requires some preparation."

Kate warily eyed the pistol still in his hand. "Okay, then, in the morning."

"Have you forgotten we can't leave the perimeter for two more days?"

"Who cares about the stupid show?"

"*I* care. I need that money."

Her heart thudded at the harshness in Alex's voice and the waving gun. Kate took another step back into the hall. "Would you please put that down?" She needed to sound firm, persuasive, but her question ended on a waver that betrayed her anxiety. Her heart told her that she could trust Alex, but her mind fired off questions a mile a minute. The attack at the homeless shelter and now this empty house and his insistence on delay frayed her sense of security.

"Sorry. I'm tired, too, short-tempered." The metal clinked against the bathroom counter, and Alex extended both hands to her. "I didn't mean to scare you."

"I want to go to the police."

"We will. But I trust your brother's county officers in Gwinnett more than any in Atlanta. Have you forgotten the police searching Underground? And the fact that they put a current detective on the TV show staff? We don't know who to trust here."

Suddenly, it felt as though Kate's pack would pull her to the ground. When her shoulders slumped, Alex hurried to help her release the load. The nearness of this man she still didn't fully trust caused tears to spring to her eyes.

"Kate." Pity thickened his voice as he spoke her name, and he cupped her face with both hands.

She swallowed a sob. "I want to get rid of this flash drive, and I want to be safe with my family."

"I know you do, and I'll get you there. Please, I'm asking you to not check out on me yet." He tried to draw her into his arms, but Kate sidestepped.

Alex moved back. Beyond the silence in the house, birds tweeted in the breeze-blown trees. Late afternoon sunlight filtered in the narrow window above the tub and danced onto the carpet in the hall. She didn't meet his eyes. Finally, he sighed. "You're right. I expected you to tell me about the flash drive. I shouldn't ask you to continue without more information either. But first, you need rest. At the end of the hall is the master suite with a separate bath you can use. I'll use this one and stay out in the living room and kitchen, give you some privacy. I won't come back unless you call me."

"Are you keeping me hostage?" She quirked an eyebrow up, teasing. Mostly.

"No, you idiot, I'm protecting you." At her measuring stare, Alex sighed. "Look, after you sleep and we talk, if you still want to go straight to your brother, I'll take you. Even if it's the middle of the night."

"Really?"

"Really."

A hot shower and a real bed did sound heavenly. Kate wasn't sure she could process anything until she'd met some basic needs, anyway. "Okay. But I'm locking my door."

He gave her a look that reminded her he'd voluntarily slept in the kitchen the night before. Where did his sense of chivalry come from? One thing she intended to ask. Alex raised both hands in a gesture of innocent intent. "I'll spread your sleeping bag on the mattress, then I'm outta there."

Intense thirst tugged Kate from deep sleep. She fought to return to an unconscious state, but the dry ache in her mouth and throat blossomed into a pain she couldn't ignore. She opened her eyes to complete darkness. Where was she? For a moment, vertigo created a sense of tilting, falling, the world unsupported around her. Then she recalled the house in the trees, the hot shower that reduced her limbs to jelly, stumbling to a room and a bed she didn't even check for stains or invaders of the insect or rodent variety. She'd even left her watch and pack in the bathroom, so she had no idea what time it was.

With wakefulness, the state of the floors became a concern. Kate paused to tug on the socks she could never sleep in and shuffled into the bathroom. She pressed the button to illuminate the watch she'd left on the counter. 12:42 a.m. She found her empty water bottle but hesitated over the sink. Who knew what was in this tap water? She didn't want to risk an awkward encounter with Alex, but he was probably sleeping in one of the other bedrooms by now. And filtered ice water from the fridge sounded so much more appealing. Assuming the filter had been replaced in the last year, that was.

In the hallway, Alex had plugged in a cheerful flower night-light that guided her toward the front of the house. As she rounded the corner into the living room, though, she discovered a quick solo trip to the fridge was not to be. Alex sprawled on the carpet beside a desk lamp, watching a TV he'd pulled off the entertainment center and placed on the floor.

At her appearance, he looked up and grinned. "She's alive."

Kate held up her water bottle. "Too thirsty to sleep."

"You're probably dehydrated."

She nodded, continuing past him. "What's with the electronic picnic?"

"Trying to reduce any flashing the neighbors might see through the trees."

"Oh. Don't you sleep?"

He stretched his arm behind his shoulder as if to relieve tight muscles. "I drifted off for a bit, but a new place makes me restless."

Padding into the kitchen illuminated by the light from the stove hood, Kate pressed her bottle against the ice dispenser. "I guess you've been restless for several days now."

When she switched to water, he replied. "Yeah, not much sleep, but I know how to deal with it. My hyper attention can be both a blessing and a curse."

Kate drank the water down and placed the bottle under the dispenser to refill it.

"Kate, come in here, quick!"

The intensity of Alex's command caused her to jerk, sloshing liquid down her arm and the front of the refrigerator. "What? What is it?" She darted to the living room, expecting a shadowy shape to be looming at the front window.

Instead, he patted the floor next to him. "Sit. You've got to see this."

"Geez, you scared me to death."

"Shh!"

Swiping her wet arm, she glared and sank down at Alex's side. She quickly realized what captured his interest. A reporter on a city interest channel wrapped up a program with an entertainment story about the season five filming of *Traces*.

The polished, female Asian anchor spoke over video footage of two bearded, twenty-something guys being apprehended by handlers. "Last night's capture of survival expert brothers Ed and Sid Woodfried in Oakland Cemetery represents the third victory in only two days by *Traces* tracking team experts. Video footage in the Grant Park area recorded the brothers as they headed into the historic cemetery to take refuge in a mausoleum."

As she continued, pictures of all the participants flashed up on the screen. "The astounding success rate of the hunters, aided by technology from The Eye Above Atlanta, begs the question if *any* of the remaining three teams stand a chance of making it even to the five-day deadline, when contestants will be allowed to cross the perimeter."

"Yasss!" Alex held out a fist for her to bump. "Half already gone!"

Before she could respond, the news report zoomed in on their pictures. "Local favorites, ex-MP-turned-SurveyCorp-security-guard Alex Mitchell and the company's own public relations manager of external communications, Kate Carson, continue to deliver clips that make up for their short length with plenty of excitement."

Kate groaned as the next bit of footage captured her "don't touch me" moment with Maude. The picture was poor, often obscured by her coat, but the audio provided ample humiliation. A real-time chuckle escaped her companion, whom she elbowed. Then, accompanied by goofy music, Alex's voice filled the living room: "Someone just fired shots at us at the homeless shelter in Eastside. Send APD officers to apprehend active shooter."

And hers: "Stop it! You're crazy."

On the footage, Kate's arm and dingy brown hair came into view. The close-up of Alex's face jiggled, then disappeared.

The anchor with her neat bun and silk blouse returned to the screen. "While these two seem to enjoy infusing extra drama into their reality TV experience, their evasion tactics have been quite effective so far. Social media can't get enough of them. They're the fan favorites predicted in all our polls to win the $500,000 prize."

As the show prepared to roll credits, Alex heaved a sigh and pressed the off button. He ran a hand across his stubbled jaw, creating a raspy sound. Maybe he planned to grow a beard as part of his next disguise. "How could they have taken that legitimate SOS for a spoof? Did I *sound* like I was kidding?"

Kate grimaced. "I'm afraid my comments made it seem that way, although I was talking about the risk of continuing the video feed, not the shooter. I still don't see how anyone else could track us unless they were using the same surveillance the handlers are."

Alex crossed his arms over his knees and leaned his chin down, tugging at her heart with the boyish gesture. "Certain security firm employees and police have access to the surveillance system on a regular basis, but I agree, most likely there's a leak. I think our key to success lies in continuing to send short clips only when our location is disguised or irrelevant."

"That doesn't give me a lot of peace. It sounds like playing with fire." Kate shifted her weight, studying her companion. The dim light softened his features. She wanted to trust him, but he'd given her so few glimpses beyond that in-control, military facade. "It's not surprising that they didn't believe you. What happened was outrageous, like a movie plot or something. I still can't believe it myself."

"I know. But I was counting on them to send help and deal with whoever is after us." Did his voice actually register a moment of weakness?

"Now that you know that's not the case ..." Kate let her statement trail off, trying not to sound too hopeful, just leaving a suggestion.

"We're so close, Kate." His dark eyes fixed on her, softening her resolve.

"I admit watching the TV report made it real, and got me a little excited again ... despite that awful frame with Maude. Then I remembered we almost got killed right after that." Kate settled from her knees to cross-legged, leaning against the bottom of the sofa. "Why do you want this so bad, Alex? Because I can't see putting our lives in jeopardy one day longer than necessary. There are other ways you could earn money to help your dad. Is it that important that it's *this* way? Are you just that confident of yourself?"

"Yes, and yes."

She rolled her fingers in an impatient circular motion. "More. I need more."

"I don't have time to make money another way." Hanging his hands from his raised knees, Alex dropped the remote on the carpet. "I owe it to him. I have to come through for them this time."

"Okay ... debt I can understand. Are you saying you disappointed them in some way before?"

He blew out a sigh and asked an unexpected question. "Ever been to South Georgia?"

"I drove through a few times on my way to Florida."

"Which is what most people do. Drive through. We say we're from Albany, but the farm is way out in the country, surrounded by miles and miles of pine trees, soybeans, peanuts, and cotton fields. Our most exciting activity is the occasional trip to kayak on the Flint River."

"I kayaked a couple of times on the Broad River near Athens. It was fun."

Alex gave her a dubious look. "I don't expect you to understand. You grew up in a bedroom community of a major university and the sprawl of a big city, surrounded by people and possibilities. But when I was a kid, all Dad could talk about was how important it was to preserve the agriculture of the area and pass on the family land. He expected his only son to attend Abraham Baldwin Agricultural College and then take over the farm, but living my whole life stuck in the middle of nowhere sounded more like a prison sentence than some grand inheritance. When the military recruiter came through right after I turned eighteen, I signed up without telling my parents. I shipped out that summer for basic."

Kate gasped and leaned forward. "I bet they were devastated."

"You got that right. Dad wouldn't talk to me for several months. Finally, he got it in his head that a short stint of adventure might shake my wanderlust, and I'd return penitent and eager to work. They never expected me to complete two tours in Afghanistan. It almost killed my mom." He dipped his head, posture and shallow breathing revealing the struggle the memory resurrected.

"I'm sure." As much as she wanted to know more about Alex, Kate wasn't sure she liked this glimpse into his pain. Compassion lowered vital defenses. But she prompted him to continue. "And then when you moved to Atlanta after you got out ..."

"All hellfire broke loose. About that time, my younger sister Jill became a teacher and got married." He picked up the remote and tapped it absently against the carpet. "When I went home for her wedding, Mom revealed how much they'd been falling behind. Since his diagnosis, my dad couldn't keep up with things, and finances were suffering. I've been sending them money, but living expenses in Atlanta are high, and it's not enough."

Kate's mind flitted back to the photo in the pocket of Alex's coat. "Your father wasn't in that picture I found."

He winced. "My dad is a hard man, Kate, but those are two strong women who now have to support him. Emotionally, as well as physically. Jill is trying to help, but it's taking a toll on her. She's newly married, and they don't make much money."

Not looking at her, Alex kept tapping the remote on the floor, flipping it end over end. Kate wanted to reach out and make him stop, but the idea of touching him opened a pit in her stomach—not disgust, but something far more dangerous. Longing?

She cleared her throat. The answer to his family dilemma seemed obvious to her, even if it wasn't easy to speak. "Have you considered moving back home to help them?"

He seemed to plead with her. "I can't go back there, Kate. You know how you feel when you're in a closed space? Well, that's how I feel in South Georgia. In a room with my dad. I hate it, but I can't change it. Believe me, I've tried. It's the one fear the army couldn't train out of me."

Somehow Kate knew what that admission cost him. Taking a deep breath, she yielded to the strong urge to reach for Alex's hand. When he laced his fingers through hers, something so sweet shot through her that her heart jolted. He grabbed onto her and let their joined fist drop to the carpet. At the same time, Kate bumped her shoulder against his in a gesture of support—the buddy-buddy type that she hoped would dispel the awareness between them … if he even felt it the way she did. "I get it."

"I'm not proud of the way I went MIA from the farm, but for my mother's sake, it's best that I stay away. My last attempt to have a real conversation with my dad ended in a shouting match. Tension makes his symptoms worse."

Kate marveled that a man she'd pegged as her polar opposite could share so many of her most private feelings. "I had problems with my dad too. He … cheated on my mom when I was a teenager."

"I'm sorry."

When he held her gaze like that, as though he looked into her soul, Kate felt such a connection to him that she wanted to share everything. "I can't believe I'm telling you this. To be honest, I didn't like you much at first because you reminded me of him."

Alex raised his eyebrows. "Thanks. Why, was he a military man?"

"No, but he was a man's man. Confident, authoritarian, kind of stoic. Alpha male."

He blinked and drew back. "You're describing my father."

"And you. Not now, maybe, but the way you came across at first."

The fact that Alex fell silent and withdrew his hand told Kate that he didn't like her comparison. He unscrewed his water bottle and took a drink. Finally, he asked, "So what happened? Was your dad sorry for the affair?"

Kate had trouble speaking past the lump in her throat. "He was. He and my mom agreed to get counseling. I didn't take it as well as she did. He and I had been at odds for a couple of years. He had very strict expectations of me, so I felt like his affair made him a total hypocrite."

"I can see that."

"He was going to a cabin in Tennessee to do some fishing—really some soul-searching—when he met a semi rounding a curve over the line. He jerked the wheel and ended up flipping over a steep embankment. It killed him on impact." She'd pictured that moment a hundred times. Her father's shock and fear as his vehicle flew through nothingness, hurtling toward his death alone, his most important relationships unresolved. It never failed to send jagged shards of pain and regret into her soul.

"Oh, Kate." Alex reached for her hand again.

Kate looked down at their joined fingers. She was opening up to the first man besides her brother in a decade because of the shared pain she sensed from him, but leaving herself vulnerable still made her stomach churn. Yet she tightened her hold and pressed on. "It was like a nightmare that kept getting worse. My mom, who had never finished her degree and stayed home with us, had to go back to work at a dead-end job. When I went to college, I swore I'd never put myself in that position."

"So you became a public relations manager at a big-city corporation." With a gentle smile, Alex released her hand, surprising her with the sense of loss.

She folded her hand under her other arm. "No … I became a writer. One of my professors saw my passion for it and encouraged me. I started working on my big novel during my senior year and finished it just after. The professor had a friend who was an editor at a big publishing house. It sounded like a sure thing. It wasn't."

"The most famous writers in the world started with a pile of rejection letters."

"I know that, and believe me, I did try. After the publishing house I counted on said no, I tried to get an agent. I queried a bunch of other publishers. But no doors opened, and the bills piled up. Not just living expenses, but student loans. When I maxed out my credit card, I had to borrow from my mom. Do you know how awful that was?" Kate shook her head. "Here I was becoming a burden to the woman I swore I'd never be like. I even owe her the job I have now. She arranged it all. Like I said, Helen was her childhood friend."

"But you've done well there. Don't you like it?" Alex pulled up one knee, shifting toward her as if he hung on her response.

"I like success, money, security. But the job is super-demanding. Helen is a perfectionist. I felt like I was running long before this show ever started. Like if I sat down for one minute, or missed a single important detail, everything would come crashing down on me." Kate exhaled a deep breath. Verbalizing her feelings made her realize just how much weight she'd been carrying.

"Sounds like success in corporate PR is a hard taskmaster." Alex spoke softly.

"But isn't it everywhere?"

"Not if you're doing what you love." He gave her shoulder a teasing nudge. "Who knows, maybe this little adventure will provide some meat for a breakthrough novel."

Kate laughed at the thought. "Maybe."

"Wouldn't it be nice to stop running from your past?"

"I don't know … you tell *me*."

"Ha." He pointed a finger at her. "Touché."

"Don't make the same mistake I did. Don't let your dad die without setting things straight, even if he's in the wrong. Otherwise, it will impact every relationship you ever have, and you'll add guilt to what you're already running from."

She might as well have dropped a hundred-pound weight between them. Alex fell silent, and Kate held her breath. Had she angered a man unaccustomed to being on the other end of instruction?

She felt relieved but also faintly disappointed when he laughed. "Wow. That got deep."

"Sorry."

"No, don't apologize. I heard you. So we both need the money to stay independent. Neither one of us wants our past to become our future."

"Right. Mom tells me I don't have to pay her back, but that doesn't feel right when she's struggling herself. And I wanted to get a place of my own rather than continuing to waste money on a big lease payment. Now, I may not even have a job." Kate bit her lip as if the gesture could hold back a flood of panic.

"Or you may have the one you're meant to have. Sometimes God uses what look like setbacks as setups."

Kate stared at him. "That's the second time you've mentioned God."

"Only the second? Well, I apologize. High-tension situations don't tend to bring out the best in me." His teeth flashed white in the semi-dark.

"Or anyone." If Alex was a man of God, it could explain why she'd never felt threatened by him. Well, except for the moment she'd been sleep-deprived and thought he was waving a gun at her. Had *she* mentioned her faith? Kate couldn't remember. All that came to mind was a string of complaints and anxiety. She pressed her lips together in a forced smile.

In a soothing motion, the rough pads of Alex's fingers slid over the back of Kate's hand. The way he kept touching her confused her. She liked it. Too much. But the events of the past few weeks bred suspicion. Did he feel the same connection she did, or had his MP classes taught him how to use a subject's vulnerability to manipulate them? And did the rawness of Clayton's betrayal and the danger surrounding them rather than genuine affection create this strong need to please Alex?

"So, now that we know why we're both in this thing, what do you say?" Alex turned his head toward hers and lowered his voice to a tantalizing rumble. "I'm just asking for a few extra days here until we go to Gwinnett."

"A few days?"

Alex darted a look at her, squeezing her fingers. "They'll expect us to make a break for it on day five. As long as no one shows up here, we could stay until day six. How bad can it be? We're comfortable. We're safe."

Too comfortable, perhaps. Too safe. Experience had taught Kate that when one felt those things, the blow was about to fall. Yet she found herself agreeing.

Chapter Nine

On the Run Day 4
6:49 p.m.

Kate's childhood obsession with Nancy Drew and Alex's MP training resulted in a shared love of classic crime shows. They'd spent most of the day before watching spy movies and reruns of *Matlock* and *Columbo*. The fact that they had a microwave available meant they ate the soup he'd left in his duffel bag rather than his MREs. He'd even packed popcorn.

Placing a queen face-down, Kate collected the cards she'd amused herself with for the last half hour after finding them in the coffee-table drawer. She glanced at her watch. An episode of *Columbo* should start in ten minutes. Her stomach rumbled. What did Alex have left in his stash? He insisted they keep everything packed and ready to go at a moment's notice.

The hum of an electric razor led her back to the bathroom he was using. Had he decided to get rid of the beard that she hated to admit she found rather appealing? The cracked-open door revealed a bare-chested Alex, his black T-shirt on the counter, a multitude of muscles taut as he leaned toward the mirror. Her heart clenching, then racing, Kate covered her mouth and started to back away when she noticed short pieces of dark hair flecking the sink.

She gasped. "What are you doing?"

"Isn't it obvious? Giving myself a buzz cut." Nudging the door open all the way, he spoke into Kate's live button cam with exaggerated emphasis while glaring into the receiver. "And since the video crew didn't believe me when I said we were in real danger, this is a good time to offer up some more generic fugitive footage—in case they haven't gotten bored to death by the hours of *Columbo* we sent yesterday."

She edged away, all that bare skin triggering nervous spasms in her midsection. Honestly, he must work out twice a day. "But why are we leaving? You said we'd stay through tomorrow."

At the disappointed whine lacing her statement, Kate clamped her lips together. She liked being able to do normal things like shower, sleep, and brush her teeth. But she could do those things at the place Lance would find for them. She liked feeling secure, tucked away from cameras and SWAT guys, even if the reprieve was only temporary. But she would be even safer under the protection of the Gwinnett County Sheriff's Department. The truth was, she'd allowed their heart-to-heart on the night of their arrival to disperse her misgivings about Alex. Now she was enjoying the time alone with him a little too much.

"And we will if we can. We've been lucky so far no one's noticed our presence, but that could change at any time. I'm glad you're here. You can shave the back for me." He shoved the razor with its plastic extension into Kate's hand before she could protest, then turned around and tucked his chin to his chest. "That little place at the back of my neck. It's hard to get."

"Yes. I see. You look like a rat with a tail."

"Thanks."

"Stop laughing." Placing a hand on his shoulder to steady the razor, Kate finished the job. He'd left enough hair so that he didn't look bald. Though no doubt he'd look good bald too. Flicking off the power, she brushed stray pieces from his neck and, pretending some remained stuck to the back of his head, gave into the urge to run her hand over his cut. "Was it this short when you enlisted?"

"Shorter, and minus the beard, of course."

"You look like you need a leather jacket and a Harley."

"A Harley would come in handy about now."

As Alex took the razor and started cleaning up, Kate glanced at the tattoo on his bicep. Two revolvers crossed above a scroll reading "Death Before Dishonor." She raised her gaze to meet his in the mirror.

"Is that for the Military Police?"

"Yes. I went through a pretty tough and rebellious stage when I left home, did some things I regret now." Alex offered a crooked grin. Not for the first time, Kate fixated on how the softness of the bow of his top lip offset his more rugged features. "At least I didn't add the skull on top of the revolvers."

"Thank goodness. It's lethal enough as is." She turned to leave but paused when he called her name, her heart thudding ridiculously.

"I don't want to ask you this, but would you consider cutting your hair also?"

Kate's mouth fell open. "Not a chance!" Was she more upset that he wanted her to cut her hair, or that he'd failed to offer the romantic comment or move she'd hoped for?

"Just a couple of inches. And maybe some blonde? I have the hair dye. I could help you. I don't have to tell you how different it would make you look to get out of Atlanta."

"No, you don't, because I'm not doing it. And you're presumptuous to even suggest it." Kate pivoted on her heel, but Alex caught her arm.

"Then I guess I also don't have to tell you that this is not a game anymore. Some things are more important than your precious looks … like surviving."

His words, his tone, polarized, and the emotional push-back hurt. As her gaze locked with his, Kate seethed, hating that something in her wanted to capitulate to his magnetic power of command. She'd thought the years without her dad had cured her of that weakness. No, she would not give in to satisfy another man accustomed to giving orders. Not even to reach past the armor of his military bearing and connect with him again.

Before Kate could snatch her arm away, Alex's expression altered. The steely glint left his eyes, and he dropped his hand. He turned away, tapping his razor on the lip of the sink, then removing the blade. "It's okay, Kate. I know this hasn't been easy for you. You're not a soldier or an athlete or anyone with the preparation for this kind of strain. You've been amazingly resilient."

Stunned, all she could think to say was, "Thank you." She watched him wiping down the sink. "How do you do that?"

"Do what?"

"Completely change tack in the middle of something. It wasn't the first time."

He glanced over. "That old me I just told you about? He still wants to rule."

"I'm glad you don't let him." Kate puffed a laugh. "I wish my dad could've learned that trick."

"Tell me about it." The statement came out deadpan as Alex put away his razor.

"Not that I have any right to judge." As her anger dissipated, clarity returned. She crossed her arms over her chest and released a heavy breath. "I need to apologize. I've been a horrible partner ever since this started."

Packing toiletries into his bag, Alex cut her an intense glance. "I know you've put forth effort."

"Really? Because being here the past few days has given me a chance to look back on my own behavior, and I'm embarrassed. I've whined, complained, tried to get out of what I signed up for, and argued about almost everything you suggested. The truth is, I've been way too caught up in being comfortable. A little pressure and I crumble. Especially when I don't look good."

She hated to admit it, but there it was. Did it make vanity less reprehensible if it stemmed from insecurity?

"What?" Alex barked a laugh. "You always look good."

Was he blind? Couldn't he see the difference between the polished image she worked so hard to cultivate in her normal life and the scraggly mess she was now? "When I have my makeup and skin care products, maybe. But I can't stand to look in the mirror since Allie colored my hair. I don't care to add insult to injury by gambling with blonde."

"You're really telling me you hate the way you look? Right now?" Brows raised, Alex turned with his back against the counter. He reached for her, edging her into the bathroom so that she faced the mirror.

Kate made the briefest possible eye contact with her reflection. "At least I'm clean, and not wearing your baggy clothes, but … yes. I don't know who I am without my red hair."

"I admit, I loved your hair."

As his hands settled on her hips, Kate swallowed. He'd said that before, so he must mean it. "I don't know why you had an opinion about it. We'd barely met when you insisted I dye it."

"We might have barely met, but that didn't mean I lacked an opinion. You forget I told you that I'd been watching you prance in and out of SurveyCorp for almost two years, and I definitely noticed the red hair."

Was she imagining it, or was he pulling her ever-so-slightly toward him? "Oh … um, thank you." Yes, those were definitely his knees brushing hers, and the warmth of his frame ignited a responding heat that seemed to come from her very bones.

"Forgive me for instructing you again, but you seem to need instructing, or at least reminding, in this particular area. You do realize your appearance is a façade. It has nothing to do with who you are."

She fluttered her hands, not knowing what to do with them. "It has everything to do with who you are. We have eyes. We live in a world where we experience most things through what we see. And we have culturally preconditioned notions of acceptable beauty, especially for women."

"And you should know that inner beauty is the important kind."

Kate folded her hands against her chest and lowered her gaze. "Yes, I know that."

Alex's deep voice became a soft rumble. "You don't need makeup or fancy clothes to make yourself look good."

"Thank you. I … appreciate that." Her face flaming with uncomfortable conviction of more than one variety, Kate wiggled in an attempt to stand up straight, but Alex wasn't helping her at all.

"I mean it. You're a very beautiful woman, with or without your red hair." His voice dropping to a whisper, he reached up to trace a strand of Kate's now-brown locks, then let his fingers trail down her cheek. When they reached her jaw, he pulled her in until she was leaning against the counter with him, inches from his face. His breath came fast, mingling with hers. "And I want to kiss you. Really bad."

His words shot a jolt of adrenaline straight to her chest. Kate's gaze dropped to that heart-shaped upper lip of his, and she surrendered to the urge to lock her own lips on it. He responded with the most thorough kiss she'd ever received. His mouth was warm, salty, his body a solid length against hers. He was nothing like Clayton, and she'd had no idea what she'd been missing. On every possible level, she'd been substituting finger foods for a full meal. The hunger that filled her escalated so fast Kate experienced a whole new kind of vertigo.

When she drew back for a breath, Alex's chest heaved under her palm. "This isn't a good idea."

She wasn't ready to put distance between them. Kate wrapped her arms around him, and to her joy, he lowered his mouth to hers again. He said a whole lot more when he wasn't talking. And she was learning a lot, fast.

Her body shuddered when a car door slammed in the driveway. They both froze. A man's voice, then a woman's, sounded from the front yard.

"Oh no, they're coming in," Kate said on a gasp.

Jerking upright, Alex snatched his T-shirt and pulled it over his head. "Your bag, get your bag."

"Did we leave anything in the living room?"

The most flushed and stunned she'd seen him, he shoved his feet into his shoes, tied them as fast as he could, and bent to shoulder his own pack. "No time to check."

Panic on the heels of passion made Kate's head spin. A second surge of adrenaline coursed down her arms and legs until she thought it might explode in energetic form from her hands and feet. Kate turned one way, then another. "How do we get out?"

"The window in the master I showed you."

She knew the one. Wide, low, and situated behind tall shrubbery, it opened onto the back yard. Kate ran to it. Together, they tugged it up and tossed their belongings to the muddy strip under the eaves.

Alex heaved himself over the ledge and dropped, silent as a cat, on the other side.

Kate jumped up and down. "Alex! I hear them at the door." A key turned in the lock.

He held his arms up. "Come on."

He braced her landing, then helped her reach the window to tug it down. Taking Kate's hand, he ran with her through the trees until they burst into the clearing of the adjacent house's backyard. They darted along a hedge row and had almost made it to the side street when an explosion of deep-throated barking lodged Kate's heart in her throat.

"Run faster," Alex yelled.

He didn't have to tell her. The sight of a muscular black dog that stood almost as tall as Kate's waist lunging around the side of the neighbor's house turned her into Wonder Woman. She didn't stop until she reached the crosswalk, and only then because she realized she'd lost Alex. She turned to find him jogging behind her, almost bent halfway over with laughter.

"You laugh at the strangest times!"

"I'm sorry. Didn't you hear me saying that dog had a shock collar? He stopped two lots back."

"No!" Kate threw her hands over her face. "Oh, my goodness, that was terrifying."

He caught up with her and drew her hands down, still laughing. "You're red as a beet."

Kate smacked him.

He slid an arm around her waist, pecking her cheek as though they were a couple making up from a fight. "We need to look as normal as we can. We should walk now. It was just a realtor."

Hope stirred. "Does that mean we can go back in a few minutes?"

"No. We most definitely should not go back, although I regret that more than I can say." Alex underscored the vehemence in his voice by leaning forward to drop a kiss on her lips, hesitating and then sealing her lips with his again.

Just as Kate pressed back, he pulled away. The rejection stung. Did he think her too forward? She'd never been the one to pursue in a relationship, but something about Alex overpowered her reserve. "You are so confusing."

"I'm sorry." Alex frowned, then a look of complete horror stole over his features.

"What? What is it?"

His wide eyes met hers as his fingers fumbled at her collar. "The button cam. It's been on this whole time."

"Oh no." Kate pressed a shaking hand to her face. "The kiss. The whole world will see it."

"You mean the make-out session? Technically, they'll only see the front of my T-shirt."

"But they'll *hear* everything." Kate wished she could melt like one of those X-Men and sink through the cracks in the cement sidewalk.

"Yeah, well, it's done. No need to fixate on what we can't change." He took her hand and urged her across the street as the *walk* light flashed. "I'm almost positive we left stuff in the kitchen and living room. The sink was wet, some lights were on, and they'll find footprints under the unlocked window. Most likely, the realtor will call the police."

Danger. Yes, they were in danger, something Kate forgot any time Alex came within three feet. "Great. So what's the plan?"

"I don't have one. We can't leave on MARTA until day five, tomorrow, and we have to alter our appearance before then."

He was right. Looking like they did, they couldn't walk up to a hotel and rent a room, even if they used their cash. Every decent lodging in this area used surveillance cameras. What were they going to do, camp out under an overpass? She moaned, but Alex shook his head.

"Let me walk. Let me think. Something will come to me."

She would trust him. She would stuff down the self-centered, panicky concerns, and give Alex a chance to figure this out. Kate trudged beside him, turning onto one side street and then another as residential areas faded into commercial. Men wearing ties in sports cars and families in expensive SUVs stared at them as they passed. Women jogging in brightly colored, name-brand athletic attire or walking their dogs gave them a wide berth. Occasionally, Alex consulted the map he kept folded in the front pocket of his backpack.

As he turned the paper to line up with a street sign on a corner, Kate jostled his arm and pointed to a side entrance to a home improvement store. "You wanted a place to change. Would that do?"

Alex stared at the row of outbuildings of all shapes and styles, doors standing open, abutting a line of trees at the edge of a spacious parking lot. A security light on a tall pole provided a halo of illumination as the sun sank on the horizon. A slow grin broke over his face. "Ingenious."

Looking around to make sure no one else approached, they darted toward the biggest one, a gray, wooden, barn-style building with white trim. They hastened inside an approximately eight-by-ten interior.

"Great. There's a storage loft." Alex stuck his head back out and gave a cry of victory when he spotted an empty plastic cement bucket the employees probably used for maintenance purposes. He dragged it inside the shed. "This will give us enough height to climb up. We can see from the window if anyone is coming."

"And if they are, we'll be spotted as soon as we try to leave."

"We'll be quick. I have an idea."

As soon as they knelt on the upstairs plywood floor, Alex unzipped his bag, relating his plans in a low tone. "Tonight, we can change into the athletic wear Craig and Allie gave us. We'll mix in with the residents. Add some dark makeup and do something different with your hair."

"I'll let you cut it."

His search halted. "You will?"

Kate nodded. "A couple of inches won't hurt."

"You sure?"

"I'm sure. I meant what I said earlier." She'd become accomplished at using her writing skill, personal charm, or physical assets to get what she wanted. Hardship and inconvenience had revealed the weaknesses of her character; now she needed to work on overcoming them. Kate opened her pack and searched until she found the spandex and poly leggings and top. "What about tomorrow?"

"I remembered while we were walking that the Braves are playing tomorrow. I knew a couple of their games might overlap with the time we could be on the run in Atlanta, so I packed two T-shirts." In the dim light from the window, Kate surveyed the red, white, and blue jerseys Alex displayed. Hers would swallow her whole. "I even packed face paint. It's better than regular makeup for the cameras. It might just compensate for the fact that we're making the dash outside the perimeter on day five rather than six."

"Did you think of everything?"

He grinned. "Preparedness is the key to success, remember? I'll go down to change."

"And then where are we going?"

"Hopefully an older motel without—"

A slamming door cut off the familiar word Kate anticipated. Alex's head swiveled toward her, and their wide eyes met. The sound of a padlock clicking into place preceded retreating footsteps. As claustrophobic alarm sent Kate to her feet, banging her head on the ceiling, he raised a finger to his lips in warning. The door of the next outbuilding closed and locked.

"Cameras." Alex concluded his unfinished sentence, then heaved a gusty sigh. "Or we could just be spending the night here."

8:37 p.m.

Alex shook his head as Kate lunged to the window. When the inset panes didn't open, she pressed her cheek against the glass. "We should yell for the employee before he leaves. He's at the end of the row."

"And have him call the police?"

"He wouldn't do that. We would say we were checking the building out."

"Yeah, with our fat Appalachian Trail backpacks. Actually, this is probably the safest place we could be right now. Spending the night here makes sense."

"How can you say that?" Kate sank to the floor, raising her hands to her hair as her chest rose and fell rapidly. "I hate small spaces! Why do you think I want out of my apartment?"

Chuckling, Alex approached her, bent at the waist. "Some people live in houses this small."

"Don't you get it? This is my worst fear. I feel like I'm gonna pass out."

Alex reached for her and, as he had in the car, pressed her head against his shoulder. He smoothed a hand over her silky hair. "Breathe slowly, from your middle. Concentrate on something else."

She stilled. "Your heartbeat."

He caught his breath as his pulse sped up. He forced himself to focus on the hum of the security light just outside rather than her enticing nearness. "Don't worry. We're not trapped. I can get us out of here if I have to, but I'd rather not damage the building." He gave a low chuckle and held her against him until her breathing slowed. "Better?"

She nodded.

Alex let out a gruff laugh. "This experience does seem to force us to face our worst fears and weaknesses."

"Mine is obvious, but what is yours?"

He pulled back, trailing a strand of hair through his fingers. "Being stuck in here with you."

"*Thanks.*"

Alex gave a weak smile. He'd have to be honest if he didn't want to distance her. "You took it the same way in Fung Chen's office, like a rejection, but you should have recognized the compliment—certainly after what happened between us at the house today. I can't be close to you, Kate. I find you too attractive. In the past, I've moved too fast and made some serious mistakes with relationships."

Kate glanced at him, then tucked her chin. "I … see."

Trying to numb the pain of his own failures, he'd left a trail of trouble, broken hearts, and vengeful significant-others in his wake, and with girls he didn't even care about. Despite his resolve to keep this about the money, he *cared* about Kate. Maybe because their partnership had forced him to actually get to know her. She was intelligent, witty, determined, and she pushed past his walls—even called him out when he needed it.

But putting all his emotional cards on the table so soon would make him too vulnerable.

Alex drew a deep breath. "I don't want to make those same mistakes with you. And that brings me to an apology I was too stubborn to give earlier."

Kate's gaze swung to him with an expression of dread. "An apology?"

"Holding your hand as a comforting gesture was one thing, but there are so many reasons I shouldn't have kissed you. Taking advantage of the stressful situation. Adding to the temptation already there. Compromising mental clarity with emotional connections. But the fact that you're already committed comes foremost. You have a boyfriend."

Shaking her head, Kate wrapped her fingers around Alex's and licked her lips. It took her a moment to speak. "No. No, I don't."

Amazement and relief flooded Alex. "You don't? But you said you and Clayton—"

"We dated a while, yes, but remember when I told you about looking for something on his computer?" When he nodded, Kate continued. "I was looking for evidence of an affair. Just after that, I found out he and Kendra—"

"*No.* The schmuck." But it didn't surprise him at all. His time in Afghanistan had taught him to be a pretty good judge of character.

"He maintains his innocence, and the competition started after that, but I know something was going on."

"That Kendra, I knew she was trouble from the first time I saw her."

"*Thank* you."

But Kate had told him she had a boyfriend at their first official meeting. Hurt and confusion warred in Alex's mind, weighting his brow. "But why did you let me believe ..."

Kate shrugged. "I don't know. Pride? You were so belittling and cold. I needed to seem independent, as if I didn't care. And I didn't know you then. I guess I also thought it would protect me."

Oh man. Oh no. For a moment, Alex covered his head with his hands. Then he let out a disgusted breath and scooted back on his toes and knees. "And it would have. Kate, I wish you wouldn't have told me that."

Kate looked as if she didn't know whether to be flattered or offended. Finally, she settled for apologizing. "I'm sorry. I thought you'd be glad."

"I am!" Alex spread his hands open. "But we don't even know what's between us yet. How can we judge it in the middle of all that's going on? Not to mention, at the end of this, I have to answer to not only your big brother but ..." He grimaced, pointing a finger to the ceiling. "The guy upstairs. So right now, I'm going down to the bottom of this shed."

As Alex felt for the edge of the loft, a smirk danced around the corners of Kate's mouth. Why in the world did she look pleased?

He fairly growled at her. "What?"

"The chivalry, now I understand it."

Chapter Ten

On the Run Day 5

"Hey." Alex shook Kate's shoulder.

She woke in an instant, shot up, and scrambled away from him, smoothing her tangled hair. "You're not supposed to be up here."

Alex nodded to the small window where morning sunshine replaced light from the utility pole. "The store's going to open. We need to be ready."

"Well, considering that I slept in this Braves shirt and I have no sink, shower, or toilet, I guess I'm ready." She did, however, reach for her comb.

Alex placed a hand towel, a paint brush, and two tubes of yellow and red paint on the floor between them. "I need you to paint a tomahawk on my face. Like this." He traced a line from one cheekbone, across his nose, over his other eye. "The blade covering this eyelid."

She drew back with a grimace. Over the request? Or being close to him? "Are you kidding me? I don't even remember what the Braves tomahawk looks like, much less have the skills to paint it over your eye." After rubbing her hand over her face, Kate reached for her water bottle.

"It's red, with yellow lacings. It doesn't have to be perfect. Most people who paint their faces for ball games are a little on the loco side."

"Comforting."

"Come on, Kate. If all goes well, today you get to see your brother and turn over the information that's been putting us in danger."

She sighed. "Fine. Give me a minute."

Alex kept a respectful distance, watching out the window. But he snuck discreet glances as Kate squirted toothpaste on her toothbrush, brushed, rinsed with bottled water, swallowed, and swiped her lips with some kind of gloss. He muffled a grin. She wanted to look and smell good when she was up in his face.

"There are some indignities I refuse to stoop to," she said as she stuffed her toiletries back into her bag.

Alex dropped cross-legged in front of her. "Understood."

After locating a grayish-colored eye pencil among her makeup supplies, Kate scooted up to him. Leaning forward, she balanced with her fingertips touching his denim-covered leg. Alex's gaze shot to her face, and she snatched the fingers away. Feather light, she began to trace an approximation of the team symbol.

He watched her without the joking she was probably expecting. "You talk in your sleep."

A flush rose to her face. "I do? What did I say?"

Alex hesitated a moment, but honesty won out. "You were calling for your dad."

Kate's hand froze, and thick lashes veiled her deep-brown eyes. A moment later, she frowned and resumed the tickly movements with the pencil.

"It was all I could do to stay down there. You're no more at peace than I am, Kate."

Alex knew he'd hit the mark when Kate's face crumpled. He didn't know what emotions he'd ripped the lid off of, but he could guess some of them from their talk at the lease house—some of the same ones he battled. Guilt. Shame. Resentment.

Before he could say anything else, Kate's expression congealed, and she whispered, "Alex, someone's opening the door."

The cheery sound of whistling accompanied the release of the padlock. Then a young male voice spoke. "There's that stupid bucket!"

They remained frozen as steps sounded below. Their eyes locked, and judging by the rounding of Kate's, she realized the same moment he did that he'd left his bag downstairs.

"Hey! Who's up there?"

Alex swung into action, propelling himself to the edge of the loft and responding in the voice that had whipped privates into obedience. "The people you locked in here last night!"

"W-what?"

"That was you, wasn't it? The one who didn't check the building before you closed it?"

A lean guy of about nineteen or twenty backed into view below, his orange employee vest glowing in the morning light. His mouth hung open as his gaze went past Alex to settle on Kate, crouching in the attic. Sudden suspicion firmed his voice. "Well, what were you doing in here to begin with?"

Kate began to explain. "We paused for a breather from our hike—"

Alex cut her off with a wave. Information was power, and you didn't give power to your opponents. Best to keep the kid on his toes, feeling a threat.

He was definitely squirming, his gaze darting between them. "You didn't call out! You could've let me know you were here."

"Are you kidding? My girlfriend's claustrophobic. When you locked us in, she almost passed out and needed medical attention. I'm interested in what your manager will have to say about this." In one fluid motion, Alex clamped hands on the edge of the loft and swung himself below without the help of the concrete bucket. He landed with a thud and stood glaring down at the younger man.

The employee raised his hands. "All right, I won't say anything if you won't say anything. Let's just both pretend this never happened."

"Kate." Without looking up at her, Alex held out his hand.

Kate tossed down her belongings and wiggled to the edge. As Alex settled her on the ground, the employee, *Blake*, according to his nametag, looked both ways out the door, then declared the coast was clear. Towing Kate by the hand, Alex glanced back once. Blake hurried to the next storage shed, probably in terror of further unpleasant surprises.

"Are we going to MARTA now?" Kate swung her arms, standing up straighter than she once had under the weight of her pack as they fell into step on the sidewalk. Alex cut her an admiring glance. She was getting stronger—in more ways than one.

"Soon. I need you to finish painting my face first."

Suddenly, she flung out a hand, craning her neck for a better view down the road. "A black SUV!"

She'd discerned the threat before he had. Amazing. Alex tugged her arm. "Get in the woods."

Branches slapped their faces, and greening briars picked their jackets as they slid down a slight embankment. At the bottom, their boots churned through a boggy area that led them deeper into the cover of the spring foliage. When the wooded area enclosed them, Alex stopped to listen, rotating in a slow circle.

"I don't think they saw us." He turned to glance at her with grudging respect. "Good eyes, Kate." As a leader, Alex had learned to give praise where it was due, but the unhappy realization that his growing attraction to her had made him sloppy dampened his enthusiasm.

"Do you think they were handlers or those scary SWAT guys?"

"Hard to tell, since the SWAT guys, as you put it, dress like handlers. On purpose, no doubt."

Kate walked around him, ticking off the possible compromising factors on her fingers. "So they either recognized us from a traffic cam, the realtor called the police last night, or the video feed is compromised like I thought, and they identified our location when we ran out of the house."

"Do you have to analyze everything?" Disappointment with himself caused his impatience with Kate, but he couldn't keep from lashing out.

She planted her hands on her hips. "Yes, yes, I do."

"No wonder you stay stressed out. Isn't it better to create a new plan and move forward rather than fretting over what went wrong?"

"Well, we learn from our mistakes, don't we?"

"Okay, yes. We need to be more careful with the video feed, and right now we're not disguised at all." Allowing Kate to enjoy her brief moment of superiority, as long as she didn't rub it in, Alex dropped his pack and sank down on a fallen log. He consulted his compass in a leisurely manner that he rather hoped might ruffle her. "Might as well sit down. We'll wait here a minute, then leave by a different route." When she continued to dance from one foot to the other, he looked up. "What's the matter?"

Kate's face flushed. "Let me think of the most polite way I know to say this. It's been about twelve hours since I visited the ladies' room."

Resisting the urge to laugh, Alex tilted his head to indicate the forest around them. "Well, you have lots of options, as long as you don't go too far."

"No way!"

"Suit yourself. Maybe it will distract you to complete your masterpiece." With a wink, Alex circled his hand around his face.

Kate sighed. "Fine, but this will be the ugliest tomahawk ever to be seen in Georgia."

After brushing off the bark, she perched next to him and cupped her hands for the supplies he dug out of his bag. Alex faced her, straddling the log. Kate dipped the tip of the brush against the end of the red tube. She looked up, scooted closer. Alex suppressed a grin. Using her free hand to steady the other side of his face, Kate pressed her lips together and started painting.

Remembering how his heart had twisted when she'd called out for her father during the night, he didn't speak, didn't try to kiss her. His understanding and respect for this woman grew in tandem to time spent with her. As her self-revelations at the lease house had affirmed, there was indeed more to Kate than fancy shoes and public image ... if he could get past her guard. The fact that he wanted to might be most disturbing of all.

He didn't pretend not to study her, though. As she completed some diagonal strokes meant to resemble the leather laces, he whispered a confession. "I like your freckles."

She blinked. Sunlight piercing the trees shot gold into her wide eyes. "You do?"

"You don't need to cover them up. They make you real, like the girl next door on a summer day." Heat climbed his neck and prickled his scalp. What was he saying? That kind of stuff didn't come out of his mouth. He didn't open the door to his heart like that.

"Ha. That's a line if I ever heard one." Kate screwed the cap on the paint with jerky movements and leapt off the log.

Alex stiffened. "I meant it. I had this neighbor—"

"Can we please go find a restroom now?" Wiping the paint brush on the bark, Kate shoved his tubes toward him. "And some food? I'm starving."

He should be glad she'd given him an out. He laughed. "Sure."

A few minutes later, their fortuitous exit from the swath of woods brought them onto a secondary street across from an old-fashioned diner. Handing Kate a pair of gaudy plastic glasses printed in geometric red, white, and blue shapes, Alex studied the business. "Put these on. They help with—"

"I know, I know. With facial recognition. An additional plus, we look like lunatics celebrating the Fourth of July in April. Can we please go over there?"

"I don't see any cameras outside. Keep the glasses on until we look around."

She adjusted her glasses. "Fine. I'm heading straight to the ladies' room, anyway. Order me the biggest plate possible of eggs, hash browns, bacon. And pancakes. A stack of pancakes."

Alex tossed a jibe over his shoulder as they jogged across the street. "Maybe if you hadn't turned up your nose at my favorite chicken fajita MRE last night, you wouldn't be quite so desperate now."

She wrinkled her nose. "I run on real food. And real bathrooms."

Kate surged ahead to the facilities. He visited the men's room, placed their order, drank a cup of coffee, and started in on some scrambled eggs before Kate emerged. Three muttering, shifting, frowning women waited outside her door. He expected her to duck her head and hurry away, but she looked his direction, and a brilliant smile broke over her face. Her reaction did strange things in his gut, even though he told himself it was not him, but the stack of pancakes in front of him, that elicited the grin.

Calmly donning her crazy glasses as the women stared at her with a mixture of alarm and disdain, Kate sang out in a cheery tone. "Sor-ry!"

Alex laughed as she slid onto the red vinyl cushion across from him. "As much as I approve of the return of the spunky PR professional, you can take those off. This place is old school. No cameras."

"Thank goodness such places still exist in Atlanta."

Kate attacked her order, washing down bites with generous swigs of creamer-laden coffee. "Oh, my goodness. This is heaven."

"You know your body performs better with frequent, smaller meals."

"I don't care. When these twenty days are over, I never want to see another Powerbar."

A talk-show anchor provided an update on *Traces* from a TV mounted on the wall behind Kate. Alex nudged her arm.

"Another team captured last night." He jerked his chin toward the reporter. "That just leaves us and one other. And I would lay odds they're not as prepared as I am for surviving outside the perimeter."

Kate's smile reassured him of her support. Then the anchor introduced footage from the contestants still on the run. "To the delight of many fans, a romance seems to be heating up between SurveyCorp employees Alex Mitchell and Kate Carson."

After delivering her last bite of pancakes, Kate's fork froze at her mouth. She whipped around to see the TV and gaped at her own face in the lease house's bathroom mirror. Alex closed his eyes as his recorded voice murmured, "I loved your red hair."

"Oh no." Kate swiveled back to face him. "Every person in here is watching that TV. And us."

As their private conversation, edited to the most romantic comments, seared the air waves, Kate's features went up in flames. She sank down in the seat and fumbled for the glasses.

Alex's voice spoke from the TV. "You're a very beautiful woman, with or without your red hair. And I want to kiss you ... really bad."

Cringing, Alex peeked over his shoulder. Kate was right. Everyone, including the people seated on the stools at the counter, stared. A little girl with pigtails standing in the booth facing Kate pointed. To the humiliating tune of kissing sounds, she cried, "Mommy, look, that's her right there! Is that the bachelorette?"

"Well, it *is* her—and Alex too!" Their platinum blonde, middle-aged waitress, Jean, returned with a caffeinated refill. She plunked her coffeepot on their table like a trophy. "I knew you guys reminded me of somebody. It was *you*. Look, everyone, we have reality TV stars right here in our midst."

Kate covered her face as the entire restaurant exploded in applause and cheers. Alex shook his head. What else could he do but ham it up? He swiveled, grinned, and waved like a homecoming king. When some old-timers at the bar hooted about his romantic conquests, he gave a clasped-hands victory signal.

"This is awesome." After completing her own enthusiastic round of applause, Jean poured a stream of steaming coffee into Kate's mug. "We're all rooting for you. So what are you doing next? Are you really going to the Braves game?"

"I'm afraid we can't tell you that, but we appreciate the support. And the refill." Smiling, he held out his cup.

"Of course, honey. You're both such cuties, we all knew you'd end up together. We're so happy for you."

"Are you going to kiss her again?" the little girl called out before her mother clamped a hand over her mouth and offered an apologetic smile.

Kate smiled back, face flushed.

Jean topped off Alex's coffee and reached in her apron for a handful of creamers, placing them in front of him. He slid them over to Kate. "Is there anything we can do to help you?"

"You want to drive us across the perimeter?"

Jean reached around as if she would untie her apron. "You bet, honey. Can we ditch Kate?"

The customers surrounding them laughed while others on the periphery strained to hear what was so funny. Apparently, the boss behind the counter possessed excellent ears, for his firm voice boomed out. "Jean, you can't leave until your shift is up."

As the employee snapped her fingers in apparent disappointment, the father of the precocious little girl turned around. "We're heading north on 85. Maybe we can help."

Alex glanced at Kate to measure her response.

She widened her eyes and nodded. "It would be difficult to convince people on MARTA that we're going to a game when we're heading *out* of town."

"I thought we'd say we'd left our tickets in the car, but a private ride would be better." He leaned over to whisper to the friendly stranger. "We need a ride to Doraville."

"That's on our way." The young father extended his hand. "Bob Newport."

"Thank you, man. We really appreciate it."

Minutes later, their bill covered when a table of fans insisted on helping out in exchange for a photo, and their belongings tucked in the trunk of a new gray sedan, he and Kate slid in on either side of five-year-old Lexie's booster seat.

When the girl gave Alex's muscular arm a nudge, he drew back in surprise. Lexie leaned away from him. "You're crowding me." Head almost on Kate's shoulder, she studied Kate. "What happened to your hair?"

"*He* made me do it." Kate pointed an accusing finger at Alex.

"Is he your *boyfriend?*" Lexie snickered behind her hand.

"Sorry." Christy, the petite, dark-haired mom apologized from the passenger seat, shoving a Disney book at her daughter. "I'm working on installing a Lexie filter, but it's more of a siege than a battle. Now Lexie, sit quiet and read about Ariel."

"It's okay." Kate smiled at her. "I'm just grateful to avoid MARTA."

Likely *she* preferred an opinionated kindergartner to public transportation, but as far as Alex was concerned, MARTA would've required less effort than Lexie.

Christy wiggled to face them, shrugging her shoulders in a gesture of glee. "And I'm excited about the story we can now tell at Grandma's."

Bob chuckled, reaching over to pat his wife's knee as he eased the car onto the interstate.

Lexie giggled, too, and shoved a picture of the Little Mermaid under Alex's nose. "You like her red hair?"

"Yes. I love red hair." Alex spoke with as much enthusiasm as he could muster before cutting his eyes over at Kate, imploring her intervention. He never knew what to do with little people.

With a teasing grin, Kate reached for the book. "Why don't I read to you, Lexie?"

"Oh, that's a great idea." With an indulgent smile, Christy whipped out her cell phone and held the camera between the seats.

"Christy." Bob groaned, his eye-rolling visible in the rearview mirror. "Leave the poor people in peace for fifteen minutes. I'm sure they're frazzled and exhausted."

"It's all right." Kate lowered the book. "Would you like to be on *Traces*? I can turn on my button cam. You may show up on TV."

"Really?" Beneath oversized sunglasses, the young mom's rosy cheeks rounder further into a smile. "I'd love that! Oh, but can we not get Lexie on there? I try to keep her off social media. You know, there are so many predators out there."

"Sure. I'll angle it toward the book and the front seat."

As they drove, Christy peeked back with awkward and approving smiles, while Alex watched out the window. But he did sneak a few glances, too, admiring how at ease Kate seemed with strangers ... especially the little girl.

"You guys have been great." Kate returned the book to Christy when Bob stopped at the entrance of MARTA's Doraville long-term parking. This time, they were careful to turn off their recorders.

Alex leaned forward. "Yes, can we pay you?"

"No way." Bob waved a dismissive hand. "We heard you guys only get a limited amount of cash. You doing okay? I have a couple of twenties."

Alex opened the car door. "We wouldn't dream of it. Besides, we're not allowed to take cash while we're on the run." Pulling on his hat before climbing out, he gestured for Kate to gear up in a similar fashion. Then he pointed his finger at Lexie. "Have a great visit with Grandma."

"She's making me chicken nuggets."

"Surprise, surprise," Christy said in a dry tone.

The family waved as they drove away, and Alex led Kate across several rows of parked vehicles. The sun rose in a cheerful blue sky, glinting off windshields and promising afternoon temperatures in the low eighties. His spirits elevating, Alex started whistling "Take Me Out to the Ballgame." Almost out of Atlanta!

As he dug a key out of his backpack's pouch, he elbowed Kate. "You're quiet."

"Well, you're whistling."

"You're still quiet, for you."

"Just … thinking about the surprising number of nice people we've met, from all walks of life. And about what life will be like after this is over." Her voice trailed off, sounding … wistful?

"Different."

"Yeah. I wonder if we'll see each other."

He didn't want to touch that one, not in the middle of a parking lot flanked with security cameras. Relief flooded him when he spotted the dark, late-model economy car he'd bought before the game started. "Yes! This is it."

Kate remained silent as they deposited their packs in the back seat. A wave of musty-scented heat rolled out, and Kate stood there without opening the passenger door.

"You okay?" Alex asked over the roof of the car.

"Just giving it a minute to cool down."

"Well, I'd feel better if you got in."

She sighed and climbed in as he turned the ignition over.

Alex obliged her by cranking the air conditioning. "So where to?"

Kate brightened and reached back to her pack, digging until she located one of the burner phones she'd packed and the tiny notebook that contained her contacts. "This is where I can finally be helpful. When I went to visit Lance before the game started, we knew I couldn't call him on the run, nor family members and close friends. He took me to visit George Jennings, the retired sheriff who took Lance under his wing when he was a new recruit. He lives nearby. If I call him, we can go to his house, and Lance can meet us there."

Alex hooted as he backed the vehicle out. He paused for a high five before putting it in gear. "That's what I call a plan. Does he have a wife?"

She stared askance at him, phone frozen in her hand. "Yes. But he's retired. So they're both pushing seventy."

"I'm not hitting on her, silly, I'm looking for some good, Southern cooking."

"I thought our bodies functioned best on small, frequent meals."

"Then I'll eat Southern cooking every two hours." He grinned over at her. "I just said that because I didn't want you to pass out from a sugar high, you put so much syrup on those pancakes."

Kate stuck out her tongue. "I haven't passed out yet."

"We're far from done, woman. I've got to keep you going."

Alex sobered as his words sank in. If he could choose between finishing this with or without her, he no longer had to think twice. Where along the way had his answer changed?

Chapter Eleven

On the Run Day 5
4:51 p.m.

On the way to the sheriff's house, they passed the exit off Highway 316 that led to Kate's family. She gazed so hard down the road you'd think she could travel it by staring alone. Alex squeezed her hand to recapture her attention. "You'll see him soon."

"Yeah." Kate tipped her chin in his direction, offering a smile. "I'll feel better at George and Mary's."

He ought to pull back. Holding her hand felt like they were a couple, a feeling that could produce an attachment he had no right to cultivate. But when Kate didn't let go, he didn't either.

The Jennings owned fifteen rolling acres outside Dacula. As George welcomed them inside his split-level ranch, Alex's tension melted away. The well-stocked gun cabinet in the den and George's calm, good ole boy demeanor might have something to do with that. The gray-haired man still wore his experience as county sheriff like an invisible mantle of dignity. Alex immediately liked and trusted him.

Mary turned out to be all Alex hoped for as well. They arrived to find her absent, Mary having run to the grocery store as soon as she learned Kate and Alex were coming. The bustling little lady, her salt-and-pepper locks cut into a smooth pageboy, soon returned with armfuls of paper bags. She scolded George for not showing their guests to their rooms and placed folded towels in the bathroom for Kate. After that, Kate disappeared. Seemingly forever.

Alex hesitated outside the door until he heard the blow-dryer turn off before knocking. "Kate? Your brother texted George that he's on his way."

"Oh, good." When she cracked the door open, the steamy remnants of bath fragrances rolled out, momentarily overpowering the savory smells of the roast in the oven. The view through the ruffled curtains of the small bathroom window revealed a busy bird feeder and a long, sunny yard dissolving into hydrangeas, azaleas, and mature shade trees. But Alex's gaze settled on Kate's face. She looked fresh, relaxed, and she'd applied makeup.

"Uh, wow. You look nice." Alex hooked his thumbs in his belt loops and leaned against the doorframe.

"You just forgot what I look like with basic cosmetics." She spoke as she plunked a variety of tubes and brushes into a small, flowered bag. "Told you it made a difference."

"Like putting sprinkles on a cupcake. You coming out?"

"Yes, I'm coming out." Kate gave a little snicker. "Worried Lance saw the footage this morning?"

He straightened. "The thought did cross my mind. I'd expect no less of a good older brother."

"Don't worry, you can stand behind me when you meet him."

Alex glared and dug a teasing finger into her side, making her twitch away with a squeal of protest. "Do you have to look like you're ready to go on a date? Anybody who sees you will figure I've fallen for you."

Kate blinked. "*Have* you fallen for me?"

"Maybe." Why had he let that slip out? Alex didn't meet her eyes as he turned away. "Guess the stress we've been under makes it inevitable that we'll either clash or bond."

Ignoring the somber expression that settled on Kate's face, Alex returned to the living room, while she went to put her things away in her bedroom. He'd barely settled in a recliner next to George when the doorbell rang.

George greeted a young man wearing an officer's uniform, his auburn hair gelled to almost-brown, who stood about the same height as Alex—Kate's brother, Lance—and a lean, middle-aged man with remarkable, light-green eyes. George introduced him as the lieutenant in charge of criminal investigations, Charles Naesmith. Alex came forward to shake both of their hands. Assuming the traditional, wide-legged, erect posture of the MP, he refused to reveal any discomfort at Lance's close perusal.

A few seconds after her brother first spoke, Kate flew down the hallway and into Lance's arms. He broke from shaking hands with Alex to catch her.

"What did you do to your hair?" Lance drew back to gape. "I was hoping it was a trick of the light on camera, but it really is awful."

Alex tensed, expecting Kate to blame him, but she reached up to ruffle Lance's gelled locks. Nothing moved. "No worse than this, bro."

He relaxed and chuckled. "Sorry. Your hair doesn't matter. I've been so worried, Kate."

Lance bent to hug her again, and Kate clung to him a minute, her fingers digging into his thick biceps. Over his shoulder, her gaze moved to Naesmith. Lance introduced him. "George told us that the clip broadcasted where Alex said someone fired shots at you wasn't bogus, that you've had real trouble."

"Yes, I have so much to tell you." Kate shook hands with the senior officer. "Thank you for coming, Lieutenant Naesmith."

"My pleasure, ma'am."

"Before we get into all that, why don't we eat?" Hands clasped, Mary made her suggestion from the dining room doorway. "I'm sure we're all hungry, and it's ready. Would you mind pouring tea, dear?" She smiled at her husband.

"I'd be happy to."

When George followed Mary to the kitchen, pointing out where Charles should sit in the dining room as he went, Alex waited on Kate. She started to move after them, but Lance caught her arm.

He cut a sideways glance at Alex and asked under his breath, but still in Alex's hearing, "He been treating you right?"

"Alex has been a perfect gentleman."

"Not too perfect, according to what we see on the TV. And I don't want to conjecture about what we don't." Stepping closer to Kate, Lance angled his body to block Alex. "You realize we don't know anything about him. Mom almost died when you took off into the night with a total stranger, a man. She's having a terrible time explaining your behavior at church. What were you thinking, Kate?"

Alex bit the inside of his cheek, trying not to interrupt Kate's exchange with her brother. Lance could say what he wanted about Alex.

Alex refused to list his own assets. He'd learned a long time ago to let other men praise him rather than himself. The urge to rush to Kate's defense, however, surprised him. He understood Lance's concern, but he treated her like she was a teenager.

"I didn't know he'd be my partner, Lance. I thought it would be you."

"Well, maybe you should have tapped out when you found out differently."

Alex stepped up, the diplomatic air he strove for weighed down by the frown he couldn't quite hide. "I have a little sister, too, and I've tried to treat Kate the same way I'd treat Jill."

Lance's impenetrable glare didn't crack as he sized Alex up. "You lip-lock your sisters in South Georgia?"

A hot flush spread over his face. He shifted his weight but didn't drop his gaze. "Except for that. And that was all that happened, on my word of honor."

Lance put a finger to Alex's chest. "Better keep it that way."

As Kate snatched the finger down, Mary reappeared in the living room, hovering like a fitful moth. "Now, gentlemen, we're all friends here. Let's enjoy our dinner and work together to come up with your next steps."

"Yes, ma'am." Lance again became all respect and boyish charm. "Need some help carrying the drinks in?"

With a quiet scoff, Alex brushed past him.

As soon as everyone's plates steamed with helpings of roast, rolls, and green bean casserole and grace had been said, George spoke from the head of the table. "I want to know everything, from the very beginning."

Mary replied with a tinge of exasperation. "Well, let them take a bite first, George."

"It's all right, Mrs. Jennings. I don't blame your husband for wanting to know about the situation he's taken under his roof." Kate laid down her buttered roll. "The story starts with me, before the *Traces* show began."

Fifteen minutes later, Mary clucked over the cold food on Kate's plate as she hurried it to the microwave. Alex answered questions, filling in the blanks since their time on the run. As various speculations flew back and forth across the table implicating Clayton, Kendra, Helen, Justin Sandler, and Mayor Barnes, and various combinations thereof, Kate dug into her warmed-up dinner.

"In my opinion, Clayton's not a schemer. He does what Daddy tells him to." Lance's face twisted in derision. "If he has any involvement, it's as a lackey." He paused as he intercepted Kate's incredulous glance. "*What?*"

"Nothing." She shrugged. "I just didn't expect you to defend him. You've always said he was selfish."

"Selfish, yes, but the order to silence you would have to come from higher up, from someone with money, power, and connections—either Sandler in the interest of financial profit and promotion or Barnes in the interest of this database."

"Those are serious allegations against the mayor of Atlanta." Shaking his head, Charles sat back from the table. His hair might have been silver, but the unlined planes of his face and the intense gleam to those feral eyes embodied the energy of a much younger man. "We'll have to tread carefully. This could blow up in more than one area. With these suspicions involving city leaders and even APD and the fact that you've crossed multiple county lines, I'll be bringing in the Georgia Bureau of Investigation. I'll turn over your flash drive to them."

George waved his fork. "I say we also go ahead and reach out to our connections at Fulton County Sheriff's Department."

"Most of them don't have authority beyond the jail." Charles frowned and tapped a finger on the tablecloth.

"True, but those who do can look into matters without interference of any APD members who may be compromised. Besides, sheriff's office guys are always more down-to-earth. I trust 'em."

"Agreed." Reaching for his glass, Lance nodded.

"Please update Amber Lassiter." Crinkling her napkin by her plate, Kate turned a pleading gaze on Charles. "I don't want to put her in danger, but her contacts outside the police can look into the bigger ramifications and bring those to light in a responsible manner."

"I'm happy to work with the *AJC*." Charles smiled at her, then turned to the Jennings. "Can Alex and Kate remain in your care for a week or two? I'll assign a patrol to monitor your property at all hours."

Before their hosts could respond, Alex cut in. "As good as that sounds, our contract with *Traces* states that once we leave the perimeter we can only remain in one location for a maximum of three days."

"Sounds like they stacked the odds against you." A swipe of George's napkin obscured part of his frown.

Mary addressed Kate with occasional glances at Alex. "It most certainly does, but I'm afraid we can't even offer you shelter for that long. I feel so bad, dear, but I have to take George into the hospital in the morning for a small procedure. Nothing too serious, but he'll need to spend the night."

"And not have fugitives on his property when he comes home," Alex said in agreement.

"Of course." Kate sent her brother a hopeful glance. "Maybe Lance has another officer friend we can stay with."

"I can hook you up, Kate, but I thought you said they'd all be on the radar."

"He's right. Too dangerous, both for the show and the real predators. I have a contact not far from here, an acquaintance from military days"—Alex shot a look at Lance, trying to emphasize both his and his friend's reliable credentials—"who became a pastor." Notable stress placed on the job title. "Although Cade Shelton and his wife Emma run a lodge and cabins on Lake Lanier, they keep a low profile because they use some of their facility as a shelter for battered women."

"Peaceful Cove, not far from Lake Lanier Islands Resort?" Charles raised his brows. "I've haven't been there, but I've heard of the place through a couple of cases I worked."

Alex nodded. "That's it."

"I'd prefer not to involve civilians. The GBI can take you into protective custody."

"By tomorrow?" Alex inquired with doubt.

Charles tilted his head in reluctant conciliation. "Granted, bureaucracy can move slowly, and the GBI will want to review the facts before getting involved. Give me a couple of days to connect my dots. I'll allow the move to Peaceful Cove, but call if there's any hint of trouble. I will alert Hall County officers of the situation before you go."

"You'll give us your burner phone numbers." Using the tone Alex imagined he reserved for rookie cops, Lance pointed a finger across the table at him. "And we'll call you the minute we have a safe house ready."

Jaw held stiff, Alex gave a terse agreement. He reminded himself he no longer held a position of authority, but he did need backup.

Lance turned to Kate. "Kate? You okay with this?"

His obvious reluctance to release his sister's care again to strangers got him a few brownie points with Alex. He forced his shoulders to relax.

In a reassuring gesture, Kate reached over and touched her brother's arm. "I'll be fine, Lance." Then she slid her hand across the tablecloth to squeeze Alex's in a brief but telling gesture.

What was she doing, choosing such a tense moment to make a statement of trust … or affection? Alex's eyes popped open wide before he hastened to jerk his hand under the table. He didn't want the cop to deck him. Lance frowned, and Mary hid a smirk in her napkin.

Alex had to appreciate the concern Lance must feel for both Kate's safety and virtue. If the situation were reversed, would he trust Jill with a virile man like Lance? No way. He decided another reassuring statement was in order. "I promise, I'll take care of your sister in every way, or die trying."

"That's good"—Lance's face split into a jack-o-lantern grin—"because *I* can promise you'll die if you don't try."

8:02 p.m.

When Lance pulled Kate aside again as he and Charles prepared to leave, this time tugging her out onto the porch, she resisted. Her emotional wires felt frayed from the fatigue of the day and the testosterone tension that continued to crackle between her brother and partner. She wanted nothing more than the cup of chamomile tea Mary brewed in her kitchen, followed swiftly by that promised soft bed with clean sheets.

"Lance, if this is more about Alex—"

"No, Kate, it's about Clayton."

"Clayton?" Funny ... the name already sounded foreign on her lips.

"What happened with him?"

Kate hesitated, not to answer the question, but because it didn't line up with Lance's typical lack of relational intuition. "Why do you ask?"

Lance tugged his phone out of his pocket and started pressing buttons. "He sent me this cryptic text two days ago, said it was urgent, in hopes you would contact me. He wanted you to read it exactly as he wrote it, so here. I hope I'm doing the right thing."

Lips parted, Kate took Lance's cell and scanned the blue bubble under her ex-boyfriend's name. The soulful cry of a mourning dove from the edge of the woods added to the atmosphere of suspense. As she read, her heart pounded.

Kate, things are not as they appeared. I need you to trust what we had and believe me when I say I care about you, and you could be in real danger. Please call me. Here's the number to my burner phone. If you call it with another burner phone, the line will be secure.

He then provided the promised number.

Kate looked up at Lance. "Why would he not talk to *you* on this secret burner phone?"

He shook his head. "I called both this cell number and the one he gave you, but he didn't answer. I haven't heard from him since this text." He scrolled up the feed and showed her an earlier message. "He did tell me right before that if I had the resources I should start looking for you. I've had a man on the scanners and in touch with Atlanta area county offices since then, but we could never pinpoint your location close enough."

"Alex is very good at evading surveillance." Kate stifled a smirk.

Lance picked up on the hint of pride in her tone. "Why does that not comfort me?"

"Yet surely you don't trust Clayton. Lance, I caught him with Kendra Reed right before I started this show. In fact, that was a good part of the reason I signed up. Even though I still don't think he'd ever physically hurt me—which is why I tend to believe someone at SurveyCorp is behind this—his credibility remains at an all-time low."

"I've never liked the dude, and no, I don't think you should trust him. But I don't think you should trust this Alex character either. I don't like his attitude." If he frowned any harder, someone could plant a seed between his eyebrows.

"You're the one who's been confrontational, Lance, not him." She pulled her cardigan closed in front and kept her arms wrapped around herself. "He has an untarnished military record with two tours in Afghanistan. He heads up security for the nation's foremost developer of surveillance technology. I'd think that would earn him a little respect."

"Respect as a man? Okay. Trust with my little sister? Not a chance. Personally, I'd feel better keeping you close by, but I didn't want to buck the lieutenant."

When Lance started to put his phone away, Kate stopped him with a touch on his arm. "Will you jot down the number for me?"

"Why, if you're not going to call him?"

"It would be smart to have it just in case." Curiosity already nibbled at her mental resolution. What if Clayton had risked his own safety to send that text, and that was why he didn't answer a call from Lance? What if he really did possess important information that for some reason he could only share with her?

"The only number you need is mine … or George's."

"Just do it, Lance."

Lance growled as he pulled his notepad and pencil from his shirt pocket. "This goes against my better judgment. You should have stayed in your apartment writing your novel."

Lifting her chin, Kate snatched the paper and stuffed it in her jeans. "And racking up bills that Mom had to pay. Why do you think I'm doing this?"

"There were other ways, Kate. You need to come home. Mom misses you. I told you I have a contact at the local paper—"

"Earning minimum wage reporting stories about town council meetings. No, thank you. If you can get these real hunters off our backs, between my contacts and Alex's outside the perimeter, we can make it two weeks, easy. It will seem like a piece of cake after commandos shooting at us."

"*Kate.*" Lance groaned her name at the reminder of danger. He ruffled the short hair on his forehead, and this time it yielded. "I should ask for leave, go with you."

"That would cancel my contract."

"Who cares about a contract when your life is in jeopardy? You've got to be the most stubborn woman on the planet!" Her brother's fingers flexed and released, flexed and released, over the holster of his sidearm—his go-to gesture when threatened. The years since he'd screened her dates in high school hadn't lessened his protective instincts one iota.

Kate slacked a hip, trying to explain. "Look, it's not just about me. Alex is my partner, and there are good reasons he needs the prize money. I don't want to let him down."

"Oh, my gosh, you really are a goner."

"I'll be fine, Lance. Alex wasn't kidding with what he said earlier. He treats me right."

"Is that why you look at him like you do?'

"Like what?" She played with a button on her sweater.

He rolled his eyes. "Like you look at the flavor of the month at Cheesecake Factory."

She was that transparent? Not ready to be called out for feelings she didn't even want to examine yet, Kate huffed. "You look at your fiancée the same way."

Lance's brow descended another notch. "Are you saying this is someone you could be serious about?"

"I don't know. He's an amazing man. A man of principles. A man of faith. And a man of action, not just words. I can see how we complement each other, and we obviously find each other attractive …" Kate turned her face into the gathering shadows to hide her blush. "But this situation is so out of the ordinary."

Lance sighed and placed his hands on her shoulders. "Well, for now, will you promise to keep him at arm's length until you have the opportunity to figure it out?"

"I promise. I'll be careful." If her feelings ran ahead of her, her all-too-recent misjudgment of Clayton's character served as a good reminder.

Kate stepped into the circle of her brother's embrace and blinked away the tears that smarted her eyes.

Lance rubbed her arms. "The minute this is over, we want you to come home for a long visit, no matter what happens, okay?"

"Okay."

"Now, why don't you go get Lieutenant Naesmith that zip drive that's causing so much trouble?"

"Gladly." Kate couldn't get back to her room fast enough.

Chapter Twelve

On the Run Day 6
11:14 a.m.

Well-rested and relieved of the burden of the flash drive, Kate sighed with fresh optimism as Alex drove them toward the lake. Their speed limit decreased as they wound through a residential area. Alex put down the windows, and Kate spread her fingers in a fine spring breeze. The silence between them felt easy, as if they were heading to a picnic date. But something niggled at the back of Kate's mind ... a compulsion to tell Alex about Clayton's message.

Finally, she blurted out an opener. "My brother told me something out on the porch."

"Yeah? I've been hoping you'd share with me what. Figured it was about me."

"No. Well, maybe a little." Kate cast him a rueful smile, which he answered with an expressive eye roll. "Actually, I might have more evidence that I was right in thinking SurveyCorp was behind the hit."

"Why?"

Kate told Alex what Clayton's text intimated. But rather than examining the facts with her as she had hoped, he fired off an accusatory-sounding question. "You didn't call him, did you?"

"No, but I admit, I'm curious as to what he'd say."

"That can wait until we get the all-clear from the cops. We have everything under control now. There's no need to call Clayton. You hear, Kate?" He arched a searing glance her way.

She crossed her arms over her chest, her cheerful spirit plummeting. "You don't need to tell me what to do."

"Don't I? Exposing us to Clayton at this point lacks any benefit. I don't trust him."

"You've made that abundantly clear."

Alex cocked a brow at her. "What, and you do now?"

Kate sighed at Alex's dictatorial tone, but her mind flashed back to the glances and comments she'd intercepted between Clayton and Kendra. The dreadful day at the lake. "No."

She turned her face to look out her window. It was high time she started making her own decisions. Alex's frequent glances her way indicated that he wanted to press the matter further, but he correctly interpreted her body language. Silence fell, and not the easy kind that had rested between them before.

At an unmarked entrance gate, Alex stopped the car and reached for a keypad. Kate leaned forward to see him press "call" rather than enter a code.

"Yes?" a male voice asked through the speaker.

"Cade? It's me. Alex. Alex Mitchell."

A hiccup of silence—during which confusion and anxiety battled in Kate's mind—preceded a response. "Alex Mitchell? No way! Hey, man. What are you doing?"

"Coming to visit you."

She poked Alex's arm. "He didn't know you were coming?"

He waved her to silence as his friend said, "I'll beep you in. Come on up to the house." The gate opened slowly, and Alex drove the car through.

"Didn't you contact him before you went on the run?"

"I tried, but he was on a ministry retreat." Alex eased the car down a narrow asphalt driveway between tall pines. "Don't worry, we have a standing agreement that if either one of us ever needs a helping hand, we'll be there for each other."

Kate sucked in a deep breath and leaned back against her seat, biting her tongue.

On their way to a classic cedar chalet-style home, they passed several new cabins with decks and grills boasting views of the glistening Lake Lanier. A two-lane dirt track rambled past the house to other cabins in the distance, partially hidden among the trees. As they got out, Kate admired a stretch of green lawn leading to a boat dock and the azaleas and mountain laurel clustering around the raised rocking-chair porch. She could stay here a while … well, the three days their *Traces* contract allowed, anyway.

A sudden, loud barking sent Kate scrambling back inside the car. She slammed the door just in time. A German shepherd bounded around the house, straight toward Alex!

"Heel, Duke." A lean, muscular man with sandy hair appeared on the porch.

Immediately, Duke morphed into a tongue-lolling, tail-wagging bundle of fur. Kate couldn't believe the transformation. Alex, who hadn't even flinched in the face of assault, reached down to pet the massive animal. As Cade jogged down the steps, Alex grinned back at her.

"It's okay, Kate. He won't hurt you."

She opened the door a few inches. "Weren't you even afraid?"

"I was counting on him to remember me. Dogs have good memories."

"That's quite a gamble." Her muttered comment got lost in the back-thumping embrace of the two men.

An attractive blonde woman exited the house with a toddler on her hip. Unlike her soldier-turned-pastor husband, Emma didn't look thrilled with their arrival.

"Dude, this is a great surprise!" Cade shoved Alex's chest as though he'd rather fight him than hug him, but his ear-to-ear grin showed nothing but delight. "I haven't seen you in what, eight months?"

"Something like that. This is … Kate."

Turning to pump Kate's hand in welcome, Cade voiced her own questions. "What kind of Kate? Friend Kate? Work Kate? *Girlfriend* Kate?"

"Um, yeah. That's right."

A rush of pleasure at even this vague admission translated into Kate's customary blush.

Cade looked back at Alex with sparkling eyes. "All three? Well, it's about time!" He rescued Alex from embarrassed silence by introducing his wife and son. "This is Emma, Kate, and our son Joshua. He's three."

"Hello." Emma greeted them with a pleasant but controlled expression. As Kate waved at the child, he stuck a finger in his mouth and stared at her with somber uncertainty. "Good to see you again, Alex. What brings you by?"

"Well, we were in the area, and the truth is, we could use your help."

"What kind of help?"

Alex squinted and raised his eyebrows in a sheepish expression. "The we're-looking-for-a-place-to-crash-a-few-days kind?"

"Oh." Face going blank, Emma glanced at her husband. "I'm afraid the timing's not good. All our cabins are booked."

The familiar pit returned to Kate's stomach. Already, they were back to this?

"Let's hear them out, Emma-bug." Cade rubbed his hands over the pockets of the cargo shorts he wore under a long-sleeved, checked shirt. He didn't look like a pastor. He looked like a Hollister model. "We were grilling, and I have a whole pack of hamburgers. Hungry?"

"We don't want to intrude," Kate said, but Alex cut her off with an enthusiastic, "Sure!"

"Well, come on, then." Cade waved them toward the house.

The man's boundless enthusiasm unglued her reluctant feet, and leaving their bags in the car, they followed the couple inside. A gasp escaped her as she took in a modern kitchen with granite countertops opening onto a dining area with a reclaimed wood table under a wrought-iron chandelier on her left. To her right, leather sofas and checked-fabric wing chairs focused toward a massive, stacked-stone fireplace. An open wooden staircase rose to a second story, while brightly colored pillows and small green plants softened the living area.

"This is beautiful." Maybe her praise would butter up their reserved hostess. "And the whole place smells like the cedar chips my grandma would leave in all her wardrobes."

Emma cast her a closed-lip smile. "Thank you. We were able to get some grant money to renovate because of my work. Our living room is used for counseling the abused women we shelter—I assume Alex told you about that—so our goal was to create a lodge-type feeling."

Kate nodded. "I'd say you succeeded."

"I've got to make tea, so why don't you men get the hamburgers patted out after Cade fires up the grill?" Setting Joshua down, Emma pushed a big glass bowl full of seasoned ground beef onto the counter.

"What can I do?" Kate stood in the middle of the unfamiliar kitchen, feeling lost.

"Oh, thanks. Here's some lettuce and tomato, if you can get slices ready on a platter."

"Of course." After washing her hands, Kate went to work with the items Emma provided as Cade questioned Alex about their adventures.

As soon as he mentioned they were on a TV show, Emma froze while holding a cup of sugar over a pitcher. "Oh no. You're not recording now, are you?"

Alex held up both hands, meaty from mashing out the burgers. "No cameras here."

"Good, because there's no way this place can end up on TV. We abide by strict guidelines to keep our state certification with DFACs."

"I respect that, Emma."

And Kate respected his respectful but unwavering tone of voice.

"I'm sorry, but we can't put you up here. If there's even a chance of filming crews bursting onto the scene, it would endanger our women." Emma plunked the measuring cup down, her fingers wrapping tight around a slotted spoon. "You should have thought of that, Alex."

"I did, but we're running out of places to go, and we're in real danger. It's not just a TV show anymore. I'm trying to do my job, too, and right now, that's to protect Kate."

"Kate?" Emma's eyes swung to her, the change almost instant. Concern and curiosity softened her expression. "What happened? Did someone try to hurt you?"

"Actually, someone tried to kill me."

When Emma put a hand to her heart, Kate almost wished she could offer a tale of a stalking or abusive ogre. But nope, all she had was a nefarious group of must-be assassins who carried sniper rifles and roared around in black SUVs. But Emma listened with focused attention while stirring her tea, nodding and frowning, as Kate shared her tale.

When she concluded, Emma shook her head, sympathetic but no less firm. "That's terrible, but we can't have those people coming here."

Both men stood in the doorway to the deck, platter of raw burgers forgotten despite the smell of a very hot grill.

"Well, we can't leave Kate and Alex out on their own either." Cade swept his hand in an arc. "Where would you even go, Alex?"

He shrugged and eyed Kate with regret. "The officers who work with Kate's brother are contacting the GBI and plan to ask for a safe house, but until we get the call for that, I'm afraid I'm down to camping at state parks as my next resort."

The wail escaped Kate before she could stop it. "But we don't even have a tent!"

"We can lend you one." Emma made the offer without missing a beat.

Oh, ever so helpful. Did this woman only have a heart for abused women? Those who had a hit out on them for trying to bring unscrupulous political and business dealings to light could fend for themselves? A hand on her hip, Kate turned on her. "I thought you were supposed to be a pastor's wife."

Emma's face went red, and she pinched her lips together.

Tilting his dark head forward, Alex stared at Kate.

"I'm sorry." Kate's shoulders sagged. "I just ... thought the living with daily fear would be over once I gave the flash drive to my brother."

"And so it should be." Cade stepped into the kitchen, placing a steadying hand on his wife's shoulder. "Kate is right, Emma-bug. You know what we need to do. Kate can sleep in the downstairs bedroom. Alex can stay in the bonus room behind our suite upstairs."

Emma straightened. "You're right. Putting them in a tent together would not be proper."

Alex coughed on the same sort of chuckle Kate fought down, but their unwilling hostess continued, her calm unfazed. "I have some house rules. You're not to interact with the women who stay at the back of the property. Talking to rental guests from the front few cabins is fine. They've been carefully screened, but they have no idea about our shelter, so please don't mention it."

"They think the women and children staying in the other cabins are other guests," Cade told them.

"Of course." Alex sounded so eager to please. For her? "We can do that."

"And one more thing. Absolutely no videotaping from the premises."

Alex's gaze swung to Kate's, and panic clawed its way up her throat. This could be the deal breaker. Extending her hands in a placating gesture, she stepped toward Cade and Emma before he could protest. "We understand."

Alex shifted his weight and cleared his throat. "Can I have a minute with Kate on the back deck?"

"Sure." Cade stepped to the side to allow them to pass.

Alex held open the screen door and led her to the far corner of the deck. He hung his head. She could practically envision the waves of intense struggle emanating from him like the heat from the grill behind her, but she couldn't stop herself from pleading.

"Alex, I'm tired of running and hiding. I can't do campgrounds and hikes through the woods and hitchhiking with strangers. I don't think I have it in me after all we've been through. We only need a week for my brother to clear things up. Please?"

His fists clenched and released, clenched and released, reminding her of Lance. Finally, his credo won out. "Survival is more important, of course."

When unexpected tears flooded Kate's eyes, he reached for her.

"For you." He whispered against her hair.

As she nestled into his arms with a grateful "thank you," Kate looked over Alex's shoulder. The young couple they'd foisted themselves upon gazed at them from the kitchen, furrowed brows betraying a mixture of curiosity and concern.

Chapter Thirteen

On the Run Day 6
6:03 p.m.

Alex expected Kate to be happy. Content, at least. After all, he'd sacrificed his chance at $250,000 for her safety ... the ultimate sacrifice, considering the whole point of the *Traces* show.

Now they were comfortable, if penniless. After feeding them messy hamburgers and baked beans for lunch, Cade and Emma had asked polite questions about Kate's background and tried to help them unpack the stress from their adventures. Then they'd showed them to their rooms. Emma's taste for neutral candles and soft greenery made her house look as though it belonged on a home decorating show. The domestic goddess had even helped them start a load of laundry before offering Kate and Alex use of their canoe.

But as Kate inserted her paddle alongside the small craft, something told Alex that the furrow in her brow came from more than the glare off the water.

"Okay." Hunching forward, Alex rested his forearms on his thighs. "We're on the lake on a beautiful evening, we're full, we're safe, and we have a great place to sleep tonight. In fact, for several nights. I'm the one who's mad about turning off our cameras to stay here. Why are *you* frowning?"

"I don't know." Kate sighed. Flipping a brown lock over her shoulder, she glanced back at him. "Did you get the feeling that when Emma suggested we take their canoe out she was trying to get rid of us?"

"No, I think she was trying to be nice." Impatience tinged Alex's reply as he inserted his paddle and gave it a push.

Kate clenched the sides of the canoe, her eyes narrowing in response. "Alex, you are far too accustomed to foreign radicals and completely naïve where women are concerned. As soon as she realized I wasn't one of her battered women, she was ready to throw us to the wolves!"

"Pretty sure there are no wolves in Georgia. Although, black bears can be a problem."

"You know what I mean."

Alex switched sides with his oar. "Her concern that we'd bring trouble down on them was totally understandable."

"My mother always said concern was glorified worry, and worry was a sin."

"Your mother sounds like a wise woman."

"She is, although I have to admit, I haven't always treated her like one." Her shoulders rose and fell. "Shouldn't Emma be the same? I mean, she is a pastor's wife."

"Pastors and their wives are just people, too, Kate." He stroked with too much force, then, when the canoe listed, let them glide. Why did she always have to make any situation harder than it was?

She rested her oar across her knees, and her voice firmed with contempt. "Well, she's not the sort I want to be like. She's the kind who give Christians a bad name."

"Like we haven't?"

Releasing a small puff of air, Kate tugged a hair tie from her wrist. With a few flicks of her hands, she drew her long locks into a messy bun. "I guess I've been pretty selfish these past few years."

"And maybe a little untrusting?" Alex suggested before guilt stabbed him. "Not that I have any room to point out faults. I can't quit thinking about the stupid money."

"I know you're sore about tapping out of the game."

"I'm trying to convince myself giving up $250,000 was worth it." Taking out his frustration on the water, Alex paddled them toward the other side of the inlet with firm strokes. Maybe Kate would get the hint and help. "I understand why Emma required what she did. I mean, they have three cabins of women and children to protect who have already escaped God only knows what kinds of terror, and a small son of their own. She's worked hard for this place."

"Hmmm. She seems like the kind of person who likes to control things." When he kept his lips sealed, she finally applied her oar, her voice carrying back to him. "I gathered from what Cade said after lunch that their church is small, and neither he nor Emma make a lot of money. Maybe she's stressed out about finances."

He wanted to help her understand his friends, not criticize them. "The rental cabins generate their main income. Her parents have helped them a lot. They got off to a slow start when Cade bailed out of seminary to enlist."

"What?" Kate swiveled around in the canoe, causing it to sway precariously. She grabbed the side with her hand and sat still but remained looking at Alex.

"Yeah, they were already married, and Cade was a year in when he got tired of being hounded by not only strangers but also his family about becoming a minister. Emma was in the same year, headed toward her master's of social work. She struggled to finish her studies, find a job near base, and be an army wife all at the same time."

She gave a slow blink. "Maybe that's why she holds on tightly now."

"I don't blame her for not wanting to risk all her hard work. I think we should've set out across country." The admission burst out of its own accord, dripping with a petulance that almost made him cringe. Was he any better than Kate, sulking when he didn't get what he wanted? Didn't he know better than anyone that once a thing was done, you let it go and moved on?

But this … nothing had been this important since he'd left the army.

Her brows formed a *V*, but before she could give him the tongue-lashing he knew was coming, a young boy on a jet ski whipped around the spit of land marking the entrance to the cove and roared past them, throwing water out the tail of his craft. Kate jerked up her oar and shook it at him. "Hey! It's a no-wake zone, stupid!"

At the same time, the first wave of that wake hit their canoe, and the little boat tipped so far she flailed her arms, then splashed into the water before Alex could catch her. Since she'd refused the orange safety vest, the cold lake closed over the top of her head in an instant. She came up sputtering.

Alex extended his paddle toward her. "Kate, grab my oar."

She was too busy glaring and splashing a pointless stream of water after the miscreant as he disappeared around the far lip of Peaceful Cove. "Get his tag number! How old is he, anyway, twelve?"

"Forget about him." Alex rowed against the waves to bring the canoe closer to her.

"Hurry. It's freezing! And I've heard horror stories about the size of the fish in this lake."

"Well, maybe if you'd swim toward me instead of bobbing there fussing—"

"I am swimming, you idiot! This is me swimming!"

He bristled at the name-calling. But seeing that she was serious, an irresistible laugh broke from his chest. "Don't worry. You're too salty for them to nibble on, anyway."

"Oh really?" Her eyes narrowed. "Since you didn't get your big cross-country hike, how about joining me for a swim?" Kate's fingers closed around the handle of the oar, and she gave a hearty tug that jerked Alex overboard.

A thousand icy needles seemed to prick his skin, and Alex shot to the surface, gasping and sluicing water from his face. "What are you doing? Do you know how hard it is to get back into a canoe without help from inside the boat?" He swam over to grab the canoe before it got away, then hung on it, glaring back at Kate. "Why do you have to act like a spoiled child?"

"Me a spoiled child? Who's pouting about quitting a game?" Spitting lake water out, she treaded in place. Or maybe that was her swimming again.

"See what I mean? You can't take criticism. You only see the faults in everybody else."

"You're one to talk. So much for your high-and-mighty Warrior

Ethos. You'd rather put me in danger than give up your precious money, all so you don't have to man up and go back to the farm."

Man up? And a low blow using his past against him, the past he'd trusted her with? A deep growl built in Alex's chest. Kate's face went slack, and she started swimming away from him.

"Where are you going?" Alex bellowed after her.

She called back over her shoulder. "Obviously, the shore."

"The shore is too far."

"I'll take my chances."

With a lunge and a couple of kicks, he managed to hook her ankle. "Kate, come back here."

She shook him off. "Don't touch me! You're all hypocrites."

With that stupid head-above-the-water, Tarzan-style stroke, she'd never make it. Alex swam back to the canoe. He managed to right it, and with some splashing, grunting, and a few choice words, hoisted himself inside. A minute later, he paddled up next to Kate.

"Get in."

"No."

"You probably can't see it for all the splashing you're doing, but there's a sign on that spit of land that says 'Private property. No trespassing.'"

She stopped and glared straight ahead a moment, resigning herself, he assumed, to an anti-climactic conclusion of her little bid for independence. Alex extended an arm. Kate swam over and wrapped hers around it. With only a little water sluicing onto the floor, he managed to haul her out of the lake. Kate faced him, dripping and shivering, hugging herself.

She mumbled through stiff lips. "I'm sorry for what I said."

Realizing why he'd gotten so angry, he couldn't look at her. His stomach clenched. "You were right. I've turned my back on everything I used to stand for. It's disgusting." He'd applied the Warrior Ethos to everything in his life except the thing that was most important—his family.

Kate's eyes flashed up to take in his face before he could wipe away the self-loathing. "You're not disgusting. Apart from my brother, you're the noblest man I know."

He was too humiliated to take exception to her comparison to Lance. "I'm a coward."

"You're the opposite of a coward."

Alex took up an oar and started rowing with a vengeance. "If that were true, I'd be in South Georgia right now, fertilizing the crops."

"Alex—"

"No need to say anything else. And don't bother to row," he said when she started to pick up her oar. "I'll have us there in five minutes. You do more harm than good trying to help."

When Kate's face fell, Alex didn't attempt to mitigate the deeper implications of his statement. No need to waste the time. Pressure always revealed what would last and what wouldn't.

Emma met them at the dock with two big towels. Alex took his with mumbled thanks before stalking off to the bathroom.

The mere presence of their hostess—much less the quiet sympathy in her demeanor—left little doubt that she'd witnessed their quarrel. Ducking her head, Kate followed more slowly. Emma didn't demand an explanation. She merely made a comment about how often teenage boys ignored the "no wake" signs and went back to mulching her flowers.

After her shower, Kate stepped into her country-plush bedroom, toweling her hair. Emma knocked on the door and entered with a pile of fresh laundry and a delicious aroma from the kitchen that smelled like homemade lasagna.

"Your clothes are done." She placed the basket on the foot of the bed. "And dinner will be ready in half an hour."

Kate's taking-down by Alex had left her in a humbled state, so her face twisted with chagrin. "Oh, Emma, you didn't have to do that. My laundry *or* the dinner."

"Yes, I did. I'm afraid my welcome was sorely lacking. I was rude, and I want to make up for it."

"It was rude of *us* to barge in on you like we did. Honestly, I thought Alex had called."

"No. It was rude of me to refuse hospitality to friends in danger. You know, there's that Scripture verse that says that by helping even strangers we can entertain angels unaware."

Kate chuckled as she drew a comb through her long locks, water spattering off the ends. "I can assure you, I'm no angel."

Emma laughed too. "Me either. I can be very ungracious when I can't see what's coming. Guess I chose the wrong business for that, hmm?"

"I'm a list-checker myself." Maybe she'd disliked the young mom because Kate saw in her some of her own weaknesses.

To her surprise, Emma slid one hip of her white capris onto the bed. "You and Alex had a little tiff earlier on the lake, didn't you?"

"When he kept going on about losing the money rather than setting out across country, I'm afraid I lit into him." She padded closer, drawn by the sincere concern on Emma's face. And oh, the feel of clean carpet under her bare toes! She'd never take such small luxuries for granted again. But the ache in her chest felt anything but soothing. "I even scolded him for not going home and helping his family in person."

Emma nodded. "We've thought the same thing."

"But it wasn't my place to say it." Kate sat beside her, fingering the comb.

"Wasn't it? Didn't he say you were his girlfriend?"

"I think he just didn't want to hurt my feelings. We've had a few … moments. But he's never really said how he feels about me."

"But it's so obvious how he feels about you." Emma shook her head, her eyes wide. "I've never seen Alex respond to a girl like that."

Kate put a hand on her chest in a futile effort to still its hopeful surging. "Really? I'm so afraid that after this mystery about the bombing is solved, we'll go back to the way things were, and I'll never spend time with him again. After all we've been through together, I don't think I could stand that."

"Have you told him how you feel?"

Now it was her turn to shake her head.

Emma picked at a small thread on the quilt. "All I can say is, he may need a little encouragement. Alex has a lot of hurt in his background from his father and some other relationships that make him keep people at arm's length. But it's not because he doesn't care. It's because he's afraid of failing."

Failure. She sure got that. Even at the notion of speaking her feelings on the subject, Kate grasped at any excuse for self-preservation. "I don't know. We sure annoy each other."

"Honey." With a twinkle in her eyes that erased every bad thing Kate had thought about her, Emma reached for Kate's hand. "I drive Cade absolutely crazy. But we're two opposite halves of a whole. That's what you've got to figure out. Is Alex meant to be your other half?"

Chapter Fourteen

On the Run Day 6
9:06 p.m.

With Joshua ensconced in bed, Cade and Emma prepared a snack tray in the kitchen. Kate reclined in an Adirondack chair near the fire pit on the back lawn, where Alex stacked kindling on top of firewood. She had gotten past her fear of Duke, who now laid at her feet, chewing a piece of scrap wood. She gave his head a faint-hearted pat but jerked her hand away when the German shepherd suddenly craned his thick neck in her direction. His tongue lolled in a slobbery grin, permitting her heart beat to resume its normal pace.

Kate employed the same caution tonight towards Alex. Despite the fact that she wore a jacket, his bare arms rippled as—clad in jeans and a snug gray T-shirt—he poked the fire. He looked gorgeous, but since their unplanned swim, he'd fallen as silent as the turtles that had sunned themselves on the lake-bound logs. And unlike the dog, no grin on the man. He appeared only a little less threatening than he had after Kate's "man up" comment. She'd actually been scared of him for a moment. With his eyes black and his wet hair plastered to his head, he'd resembled a death skull risen from the depths of the lake.

"My, the stars are pretty." Leaning her head back, she gazed up between the trees.

He grunted in answer.

"So good to get beyond the city lights and remember what's out there."

"Mm-hmm."

Kate let out a gust of air. Alex's silence had strained dinner and now threatened to ruin a good bonfire. "Are you still mad at me? Because

I've already apologized."

She could have roasted a marshmallow before he answered—if she had one.

"No, I'm not mad at you. I'm taking some time to process what you said."

"One processes in the confines of one's room, not in the company of others." She sat forward, making her tone as gentle as possible. She even allowed a ripple of a laugh, low, like an undercurrent. "You sounded like a caveman tonight. Please don't make your friends sorry they took us in."

Alex glanced up, the light of awareness in his eyes fading to regret. "You're right again. I'm sorry. And I'm sorry I reacted earlier like I did. A lot is hitting me right now." He winced. "Did I really come across that bad? I thought I covered it."

Cade's voice boomed from the hill sloping down to the lake. "I've got something guaranteed to cheer the mopes out of you, Alex Mitchell!" He proceeded toward them with a big grin and a tray of drinks and food packages.

Alex and Kate both laughed, while Alex covered his face with his hand.

"What? It's already working?" Cade paused to run a hand down his fit physique. "Or is it the delight of my mere presence?"

Emma followed with a couple of folding trays under her arms. "Oh, you, quit preening and set the s'mores up."

Kate turned to Alex in surprise. "S'mores? Is that your weakness?"

"One of many."

"Chocolate. I can deal." She leapt up and approached the table, rubbing her hands together. "Although I can't think where we're going to put it after that incredible lasagna and salad we had for dinner, Emma."

"Oh, we'll find a nook to stuff it in. And men this size, let me tell you, they eat like they're hollow from head to toe. I'm dreading the day Joshua catches up with his daddy."

"Joshua! Just wait, Emma-bug. We're going to have a whole quiver full of hearty boys." Reaching out to run his hand down her arm, Cade gave her a suggestive wink.

Emma responded with a snort. "We'll see about that."

When four marshmallows roasted on four metal sticks over the popping fire, happiness rolled through Kate. This felt right, like a double date with good friends. Did Alex feel it, or was he still focused inward? She met his eyes, but he seemed to take her questing look as a prompting to apologize.

He let out a ragged sigh and looked at their hosts. "I'm sorry, guys. I know I've been a jerk this afternoon."

Cade manfully shouldered part of Alex's admission. "It's okay. I'm always a jerk for two or three hours after Emma takes me to task too."

"Well, you probably at least go off by yourself to pout. Guess I still have some socialization issues to work on."

Emma rested her forearms on her knees and grinned at Alex. "I can help you with that. Let's set an appointment for the morning."

Kate offered an appreciative chuckle, but Alex hung and shook his head. He sighed. "Truth is, I could probably use a good 'Come to Jesus' from both of you. I'm realizing I've had some priorities out of order, and I'm a really bad loser. And now that I know no big payment is forthcoming, I've been wrestling with what to do about my dad."

"Ever think this was exactly the way things were meant to be?" As a spark popped too close, Cade moved his chair away from the hottest part of the fire and repositioned his stick. "So you wouldn't take the easy out?"

Alex shifted, reeling in his marshmallow for examination. "Yeah, but you guys all know how he is … well, as best you can without actually meeting him. I can't just move back in. We'd blow the roof off the house. Ow!" A premature attempt to remove the gooey white candy resulted in him sucking on a burned finger.

Kate slid over and offered him the graham crackers from her plate.

"Thanks." With a doleful glance, he accepted her peace offering.

Emma flitted over to press a square of chocolate on top. "Maybe you could live nearby, like in Albany." Standing back, she nibbled the blackened end of her own marshmallow. "Mm, crunchy. Perfect. I am a s'mores aficionado."

"You could hire someone to help out at the farm, like a manager, but you'd be close to make sure things were getting done." Cade admired the results of his efforts, a marshmallow browned perfectly on all sides, before lifting his gaze to Alex again. "Ever considered a career in law enforcement?"

Alex turned the same look on his friend that he had on Kate. Miserable. He was miserable.

"What? You too good for that?" Cade's brow furrowed.

"Naw, man, it's not that."

The preacher wasn't buying. "I get it. You're afraid you'll get bored to death watching for traffic light infractions on back roads. Like I thought being a preacher was too unglamorous and humble. Well, I can tell you, you better be sure you're supposed to be doing what you're doing because when you're not, nothing works out right. And I do mean *nothing*."

"Don't let him get on his high horse." Emma rested a hand on her hip. "I practically had to insist he leave the military by issuing him an ultimatum. He liked his tough guy image a little too much. It took a whole series of setbacks before he stopped running from his true calling."

Kate completed her s'more but stared at it without taking a bite. There were those setbacks again that Alex had talked about at the lease house—the roadblock to her career, the disaster of this reality show. The hole-in-her-gut feeling told her she needed to apply Emma's words to her own life, her writing. When she'd lost herself in typing away at her novel, she'd enjoyed a sense of peace and purpose she hadn't found since.

"You okay, Kate?"

A flash of affection for Alex stirred Kate back to life. That he noticed the tiniest lapse in response from her even when he was upset himself warmed her even more than the fire. "Yes. Just thinking maybe that message was for me."

He pressed his lips into a smile. "Yeah, because I'm not running from a county sheriff's office or beat cop duty, bro," he said to Cade. "I'm running from my dad."

The way Alex's voice choked up on the last word, Kate reached over and took his hand. Emma smiled at her in the semi-dark, sweet and approving. How had she not liked Emma? She appreciated her more now than if Emma had come across as impossibly perfect from their first meeting.

Emma shifted towards Alex and spoke softly. "Maybe he's not going to be the same dad he was. Alzheimer's changes people."

No humor lightened Alex's huff of a laugh. "Yeah, it may make him worse."

Cade didn't offer false hope about the prognosis. "It may, but God is bigger than Alzheimer's, and he's bigger than your dad. You know that power trip we'd get in the military when we completed something we thought we couldn't? When we came out of a militarized zone without any casualties? Well, God can give us strength to face the things that might otherwise break us ... or make us run."

"Man, stop." Alex thumped his chest with his free hand. "Everything you're saying, it's hitting me right here like a load of bricks. I just don't know if I can do it. Being around him is the worst thing in the world for me. It's like poison."

Kate rubbed Alex's shoulder, feeling his pain like a palpable force. He dropped his head and ran his hands over his dark hair.

"I don't want to be like him," Alex muttered in a ragged voice. "And from what Kate said to me recently, I'm well on my way."

She started to make amends, but, onto something she couldn't quite sense, Cade shushed her with a gentle wave. "Then you've got to stop holding people at arm's length. Because that's what your father does, right? You can never please him? He comes across cold, aloof?"

Alex nodded.

"What happened with the woman in Afghanistan didn't help. Have you been able to let that go, man?"

Alex shook his head in a gesture of slow, agonized indecision. Kate leaned forward, willing him to answer. Did this have to do with Alex's friend Carver had mentioned at the homeless shelter? Something about an explosion.

Emma startled her by jumping up. "Kate, I forgot something in the kitchen. Can you come help me?"

Hand still on Alex's shoulder, she parted her lips in exasperation. Why would she leave him now, of all times? But when she frowned at Emma, her hostess gave an emphatic tilt of her blonde head toward the house. Fine.

As she followed Emma up the hill, Cade moved closer to Alex, and she heard him say, "Time to let go of that heart of stone, brother."

Emma started chattering, not letting Kate eavesdrop further. "So I have stuff for mountain pies. You know what mountain pies are? You've got to have the mountain pie makers, the long tong things you put buttered bread in, but inside the bread, you can do pizza stuff, ham and cheese, even pie filling."

"Uh-huh." Kate looked back toward the campfire as a whippoorwill released its mournful tune. She kept hearing Cade's admonition in her head. Her heart was hard, too, determined not to be like either of her parents, determined to take care of everything without any help.

"Apple, cherry, peach." Emma continued, sounding an awful lot like someone familiar. Forrest Gump—that was who. "Oh, peach is my favorite! I'm so glad Joshua is asleep. He gets a terrible sugar high. But the men, they'll be wanting more than dessert stuff. And I'd just as soon they don't ransack my kitchen later. I can't believe I forgot to take the stuff down there."

Kate stood in the door of the kitchen without seeing anything inside. Emma started bustling around but then seemed to realize she'd invited a zombie into her home.

"You okay?"

"What's going to happen down there, Emma?"

Emma put a hand on her hip. "Hopefully, a man talk. That's why we needed to clear out. There are moments our guys don't need us to coddle them. They need to face the hard truth."

"And once they do?"

"Why, they go out into the world and slay the dragons. And when they mess up, as they inevitably will, we're there for them."

A shiver ran through Kate. She wanted a man like that. She wanted a partnership like that.

Emma took Kate's response for fear. She brushed her hand down Kate's arm. "It'll be all right. They'll talk it out, and Cade will pray with him if Alex will let him. You came to the right place. I was just too stupid and selfish to see it at first. But now, I'm feeling really hungry again. Help me find the lunch meat?"

"Sure."

A few minutes later, Kate left Emma buttering bread while she set out down the hill with the campfire implements and a plate of meat and cheese. Maybe Emma was right. She'd seen a brokenness in Alex tonight he'd barely let her glimpse before. If he could make a stride toward reconciling the pain of his past—show his commitment to working through things in important relationships—she could make a stride toward Alex, couldn't she? She would try to talk to him tonight.

As she approached, the men, with their backs to her, continued deep in conversation. Kate slowed and softened her steps, straining to listen.

"Part of softening that heart might be letting Kate in." Cade nudged Alex with his knee. "She seems like a great girl, Alex, and I can tell you like her."

"I sure do." The enthusiasm in Alex's voice brought a smile to Kate's face and her feet to a halt.

"Then you think you may keep seeing her after the dust settles?"

Alex lifted a shoulder. "Maybe. Depends."

"On her?"

"On what she expects. Let's look at this realistically. How long have we spent together? It feels like a month, but it's been what—maybe a week?"

Kate's mouth went dry, and she swallowed hard. Had it really only been that long? But they had been together twenty-four-seven, and they'd conquered challenges most couples would never even face. Didn't that count for something?

Alex shook his head and started drawing in the dirt with a long, slender stick. "Yeah, Kate does seem special, but you know how clingy girls can get, even under normal circumstances. And this has been far from normal. Not to mention what we just talked about—I've got a lot to settle before I think about any big commitment."

Kate's hands started shaking so bad she thought she'd drop the platter. Alex thought her clingy. He thought she was like Mom had been, relying on Dad when he wasn't reliable because she was needy, desperate, and ill-equipped. Well, she'd show him different.

"Think about it, okay? Don't be afraid to give her a chance."

Kate almost stumbled as she turned and ran up the hill.

Chapter Fifteen

Kate stared at the TV as Alex rummaged through one of Cade's tackle boxes. The young pastor had granted Alex access to his fishing supplies while he went to his church office.

Alex glanced up, a plastic lure in his hand. "Why didn't you come back to the fire last night?"

"I felt sick to my stomach."

He cast her a searching glance. "You better now?"

"Much." Kate couldn't keep sarcastic emphasis from seeping into the word.

"Emma said you practically ran off. She said it seemed like something upset you."

"Nope."

With a sigh, Alex put down the fishing lure. "Okay, I'm usually the one with the one-word answers, especially when I'm upset. What's going on, Kate?"

"Everything's fine, Alex." If he was going to use her name as a power handle, she could do the same. But she made sure his came out impersonal, flat, as if she spoke to a stranger. "It's the way it should be. We'll be out of this soon and able to return to our real lives."

He came over and dropped down next to her on the sofa, leaning over so that avoiding eye contact became almost impossible. "Emma was afraid you'd overheard something I said to Cade that you might have taken the wrong way."

"No misunderstandings here. I read you loud and clear, commander. Now, will you please sit back so that I can see the end of this movie?"

Kate flashed a fake smile before waving the remote.

Alex snatched it out of her hand and mashed the pause button. "No, we need to hash this out because I can't handle the return of the red-haired vixen."

Kate looked at him. "There's no vixen. Vixens are alluring, tricky. I'm not trying to allure or trick you. Once this little adventure is over, you don't have to deal with me again."

"I *want* to deal with you. I like you, Kate, a lot. I hope our friendship can continue after this, if we both stay in Atlanta. I've just got a lot to figure out."

Friendship. That was what he wanted? She forced the tears back, forced her voice to remain flat. "Okay."

"That's it? *Okay?*"

"Yes. I'm agreeing with you. That's exactly what I think too."

Alex let out a heavy sigh. "Look, I'm sorry I let things get out of hand. From my time in the military, I knew better. People bond in high stress situations all the time, only to realize later that they have no real connection and nothing in common. Don't tell me you haven't worried about that too. I mean, I'm about as opposite from Clayton as I can get."

"Agreed." Yes, he was opposite, but she'd come to believe he was opposite in a good way. Now she wasn't so sure. His words sat like a hundred-pound boulder on her chest. Kate picked the remote up and held it out, propped up on her knee, staring straight ahead. She waited, but he didn't leave.

Instead, he stared at her as though he wanted to strangle her or kiss her—she couldn't tell which. Finally, he let out a cry of frustration that made her flinch. "What do you want from me, Kate?"

Kate scooted over on the cushion and smoothed down the leg of her shorts. He might be attracted to her. He'd admitted as much. But he thought they weren't a good match. And now that he'd said "friendship," she could never share the emotionally intimate things her stupid heart craved. "Nothing. I don't want anything. I came into this perfectly able to take care of myself, and I go out of it the same way.

No, better. I did learn some things from you. You reminded me that letting God and certain other people into my life makes me stronger, not weaker. So thank you." She met Alex's tormented dark gaze. Why did he think he had a reason to look tormented? "Now go fishing. We're good."

Alex jerked up the tackle box and pole and stormed out the deck door. Kate sat there a minute, no longer caring about the end of the movie. Her heart hurt. It might hurt a little less if she'd been wrong about only one of two men she'd fallen for. Sliding her hand into her pocket, she fingered the little slip of paper from Lance's notepad. Maybe, just maybe, she'd been wise to keep it.

A car door slammed, and Kate went to the window. Beside one of the smaller cabins, a driver loaded luggage into the back of a minivan. Emma hugged a young Hispanic woman and a small girl, keeping her arms around them a minute and bowing their heads together as if praying. Now there was someone whose life mattered.

Kate's heartbeat sped up. Maybe she hadn't achieved success with her novel because it wasn't the one she was meant to write. Maybe it wasn't the writing itself, but the subject matter that hit the road block. In her youthful manner typical of disdaining Bonnie's hard, humble work, Kate hadn't even asked her mother's opinion. Much less God's. Buoyed along by the praise of men, she'd gone with the first romantic and exciting plot line that entered her success-starved brain.

She'd wasted so much time clamoring for success and security. Well, Kate was tired of wasting time. She'd been wrong about a lot of things, and there were many amends to make. She also had someone who could help her get on with her "real life" right now.

5:22 p.m.

Alex spent the afternoon on the dock. After he grabbed a sandwich at noon, Emma told him Kate had volunteered to clean the vacated cabin and planned to eat while she worked. He offered to help with chores, too, but their hostess sent him back out, telling him she'd clean any fish he caught for dinner. Most likely, she sensed his restlessness and wanted him out from underfoot. She and Cade were probably tired of providing free counseling sessions.

He'd hurt Kate, but how was he supposed to trust his feelings for her in the midst of trying to protect her life? And when he considered the future, the crushing conviction that he had to deal with the problems with his parents weighed heavier than anything else.

As he headed back to the house, a cry from Emma sent Alex running up the deck steps. He found her frozen over the gate monitor. The camera showed two black SUVs waiting to enter, the man leaning out the window of the first vehicle indistinguishable due to a hat and dark glasses.

"They're asking for you." Emma clasped her hands in front of her chest as Kate entered behind Alex.

Kate dropped her bucket of cleaning supplies with a thud. "Who is?"

"He showed a badge. What if he's really a cop? Or FBI?" Emma pressed a hand to her heart. "I could get in big trouble for denying him entrance."

"He's not a cop." Alex leaned closer to the screen, his heart clenching with dread and dismay. "These are the same people who've been tracking us."

Kate licked her lips. Why did she look hesitant rather than panicked?

Emma straightened her shoulders, voice firming with resolution. "I'll stall him. I'll ask for his ID number and call it in. If it doesn't check out, I'll call the sheriff. But you should go now."

"How?" Kate's arms hung by her sides. She looked limp enough to slide onto the floor.

"The ski boat." When Alex nodded, Emma reached in a drawer and tossed him a set of keys. "Drive it across the lake to the Mueller's boat house on Six Mile Creek and leave it there. They won't be home, but I can call some friends from Cumming to pick you up on Highway 306.

You know it?"

"No, but I'll find it."

"Let me give you directions."

"A map would be better. Kate"—Alex swung around to meet her blank expression—"go get your stuff."

Not a twitch of animation. "What if the men at the gate aren't a threat? We will have left for nothing."

What was wrong with her? Was she so tired of running she was ready to give up, no matter the consequences? Well, he wouldn't give her that option. Alex barked out a command in his best officer voice. "We're not chancing it. Now go!"

As she stumbled off to the guest room and Alex ran up the stairs, Emma spoke into the monitor in a remarkably calm, almost impatient, voice, so clear it carried to the second floor landing. "I'm sorry, but I know you're not with the county sheriff's office. I'm going to have to ask for your badge number. Then you'll have to wait while I look up the appropriate number to call. What agency did you say you were with?"

When they returned with their heavy packs, Emma hurried over with wide eyes. "He wouldn't tell me who he worked for. He signaled the driver behind him, and both vehicles roared off." Her breath came shallow, and the fingers she placed on Alex's arm trembled. "Alex, I'm scared. You were right, these people aren't legit. I'm afraid they're going to try to come on the property illegally."

"I need you to call the retired sheriff in Gwinnet I told you about." Alex handed her the number he'd jotted down for that purpose. "Tell him what happened so he can alert his associates here."

She nodded, took the slip of paper, and then handed Alex one, along with a folded map. "I'll also tell him that once you cross the lake, you'll be in Forsyth County. They'll need to send deputies. Here's the number of our good friends, the Johnsons. They can take you to the sheriff if the officers don't locate you first."

"I'm sorry to put you in this kind of trouble. It's exactly what you were afraid of." Alex offered his friend's wife a quick half-hug.

"It's okay. I see now you really did need help."

Kate also hugged Emma. "Thank you for all you've done. I hope we can see each other again some time."

"Me too." She followed them to the deck door, calling Duke. As soon as he bounded up with tail wagging, Emma told him to heel in a voice that let him know she meant business. He sat down at her feet and snapped to attention.

Alex felt slightly better knowing the German shepherd would guard Emma and Josh with his life until Cade or the police arrived.

"Oh, wait." She called after them as they descended the porch steps. "I forgot something important. When that driver first buzzed in, he gave a name of someone in the back seat of the SUV. He only got mad and started waving his badge around after I said we didn't know anybody by that name, or yours."

Alex paused, turning on the lawn. "What name?"

"Clayton Barnes."

Chapter Sixteen

On the Run Day 7
5:46 p.m.

"What have you done, Kate?"

The agonized question rang in her ears, full of betrayal, even after Alex dragged her with tears of fright and regret running down her face to the dock and started the engine of the ski boat.

As they pulled out, ratcheting the already impossible tension up another notch, he pointed out a spy drone hovering above the trees on the Sheltons' property. "We can only pray it doesn't catch sight of us and that its range doesn't reach the other side of the lake."

Kate kept repeating that she was sorry, but he shook his head. Under a sullen sky that promised rain, he eased the craft out onto the quiet gray waters of Lake Lanier.

Then the torrent started, not of water, but of words. Questions, shouted over Alex's shoulder as he steered at the helm. "Why would you trust him? Why would you call him? Why couldn't you wait for your brother to do his job?"

As they bore left past a chain of small islands and pressed into a long finger of the lake, Kate placed both hands on her temples, doing little to hold back her whipping hair or her painful thoughts. She dragged in shallow breaths past the searing pain in her chest. "Because I didn't want to believe this about him! I believed he cared for me. I used the burner phone. It shouldn't have been traceable."

"Well, something was. Did you call from inside?"

She shook her head. "The deck."

"If a speed boat went by in the distance, even the smallest sound can be magnified, calculated."

"I'm sorry! I'm sorry, okay?"

Alex throttled back speed to pass between the supports of a green, steel-truss bridge. He read the sign aloud, "Browns Bridge Road," then turned an anguished expression on her. "I just don't understand, Kate."

"How can you look upset? Surprised? After the way you acted toward me?" She sank into one of the vinyl swivel seats.

Alex slanted her another look. "You called him to get back at me? Was that it?"

"No, that would be petty. I called him because I realized I'd been wrong about so many things, you included. I wanted to believe Clayton. He told me he cared about me, that I was in danger. He said nothing happened with Kendra. He invited her over to the lake that day because he wanted to dig for information about whether SurveyCorp had something to do with the bombing. Some things Kendra had said, how hard she pressed his father to agree to The Eye, and how fast they'd wanted a decision and an announcement after the bombing, made him suspicious."

He stared straight ahead, his jaw firming. "And what did you tell *him*?"

"Only that I had concerns as well after I noticed the mismatch of the time stamps on the press release. He got all excited. He said if I had documentation of that, it could help implicate Kendra and Sandler." She sat forward, hoping to soften him. "I didn't—I didn't verify that I did. I acted vague. He wanted to pick me up and compare notes, then go to the police together."

Alex motored them left, she assumed toward the inlet of this Six Mile Creek. Homes with docks now crowded on either side of the strip of water they traversed, and fishermen cast bait out along the shores. One waved, having no idea pursuit rather than pleasure brought them out onto the lake today. Kate waved back.

"Well, he obviously assumed you have the info with you. I can't believe all he had to do was feed you a few lines, and you trusted him."

She dropped her hand, Alex's disparaging tone stinging her to the core. "The way I'm trusting you? And I've known him much better and much longer."

At that, his head whipped around again. "Are you calling my integrity into question? After the way I've treated you this past week?"

"No, not your integrity. Just saying, there's so much I don't know about you."

Alex slowed the boat, surveying each dock now. "Like what? What do you want to know?"

His willingness to talk showed a softening, but what she wanted to say would open a can of worms. She should brush it off rather than add tension and distraction, but the unease which had been bubbling since Clayton peppered her conscience with doubts burst out of her. "Like ... why you even left the military. It obviously wasn't to go home."

"Is this coming from your upstanding boyfriend too?"

She stiffened. "As you well know, he's not my boyfriend."

"The Muellers' dock!" Alex pointed to a homemade sign.

As he angled them alongside the platform, Kate braced herself, digging her fingers into the padded seat. "Clayton did say your past was part of the reason he wanted to pick me up."

She was doing it again, reacting to Alex's disapproval by hurrying to put more distance between them ... to try to make it look like she didn't need him. She couldn't seem to stop herself.

"What the blazes are you talking about?"

The question came out extra loud as Alex cut the engine, causing both of them to look around to make sure no one lounged nearby. The shore was clear. Satisfied, he bent to uncoil a rope, not giving Kate a chance to answer. "Jump on the dock, and when I throw you the line, wrap it as tight as you can around the mooring."

She did as he instructed although it was more of a "stumble up" than a "jump up." Alex tossed their belongings onto the dock before climbing out of the boat himself. He looked around until he spotted a brown plastic storage bin. "She said they wouldn't be home, to hide the key under here."

After he completed that task, they loaded up under the awful packs. Kate glanced around. "Now what?"

Alex led to the end of the dock, then jerked his head to the left. "We continue this way until we reach the opening of the creek, then follow the water up past a mill ruin and a dirt road to Highway 306. I'm to call Emma's friends from the road. She'll have them up to speed." He stopped and speared her with an accusing stare, shattering her hope that he'd move on with the task at hand. "But first, tell me why Clayton wanted to pick you up, besides to probably *kill* you."

The cold emphasis on the word caused reality to set in, filling Kate's eyes with tears. "I can't believe that. I won't believe that."

"How else are you going to explain those SUVs at Emma's gate?"

"I don't know." A cauldron of emotion in her chest clogged her throat, threatening to overflow in tears. She swallowed hard. "Can we please just talk about this later?"

"I want to know why Clayton wanted you away from me, besides simple jealousy."

Kate tucked her fingers under her pack's shoulder straps. "He said that you left the army after some sort of incident with a female private. Was that"—she bit her lip—"what you referred to when you said your past included transgressions with women?"

Alex's mouth fell open. "You think I'd be stupid enough to get involved with a female recruit? Or worse, to harass her in some way?"

"I don't know. No. Because of what Carver said back at the shelter, I thought maybe ..." That maybe he'd fallen in love with a woman in the army, then she'd gotten killed, although Kate couldn't quite say that out loud, especially since he turned and started walking west.

Pressing her lips together, she scrambled to keep up, skirting another dock before reaching the cover of woods. A row of well-manicured homes and cottages perched on elevated green lawns to their right, with pathways rambling down to the water. Kate tried to scan for guard dogs while also conducting a visual sweep of the underbrush. Her mind darted over the potential threats lurking there: ticks, spiders, poison oak and ivy, *snakes*. But mostly, she thought of what she could say to break the awful silence. Why couldn't she stand to disconnect from this man?

Finally, they reached an inlet where a slow, muddy creek emptied into the lake. Ferns and water plants grew heavy along the red clay banks.

"This is it." Surveying the point where the water source emerged from the trees, Alex firmed his jaw. "I'd recommend taking our shoes off and wading."

"What?" Adding leeches to the list of possible predators? Kate recoiled, drawing her shoulders up to her ears in a cringe of horror. "I'm not wading in that."

"It would make us harder to track, especially if they have dogs."

She hadn't considered that possibility. Her heart sank. She licked her lips, weighing the two different levels of threat.

Before she could reply, Alex sighed and started picking his way up the bank. "Never mind."

"Wait." When Kate touched his arm, he turned. The handsome angles of his tan face against the army green hat and camo jacket he wore made her heart lurch. "I'm sorry. I didn't mean to question your honor. You've given me no reason to."

"It's okay." He turned and started walking, but the flat tone of his voice left her unsatisfied.

"I admit I was curious." Kate watched the bank for slithery creatures as they left behind evidence of the residential area. "But it's not any of my business."

He answered over his shoulder. "I don't have anything to hide, Kate. I'll tell you whatever you ask. It just bothers me that you'd listen to Clayton."

"I guess that's because I still can't believe he'd harm me. There's got to be another explanation."

"When you figure it out, let me know."

"I just want to talk to him face to face. I'm sure then that everything will be—"

"Shhh!" Freezing in place, Alex flung his arm back in her direction.

Kate almost stumbled into him. Stopping with a hand on his broad back, she was so busy listening over her thudding heart for the baying of tracking hounds that she almost missed the low-pitched whirring in the distance. She gasped.

"Drone." Alex whipped his head back and forth while she tried to spot the flying surveillance machine. He took her hand and pulled her upstream and uphill toward a small eruption of boulders at a thick cluster of trees. "Quick, get next to the rocks."

Kate followed his lead, crouching down in last fall's leaves as he fumbled in his pack and yanked out the strange Mylar blanket she'd noticed the day they went on the run. "We need to blend in with the thermal clutter to throw off any infrared sensors. Lie down next to me between these rocks."

Though she had no idea what he was talking about, the humming had gotten louder, so she did as he ordered without question or protest. With their packs at their feet, they lay prone, and Alex spread the material over them. She breathed in shallow gasps as she heard the drone fly over.

When she wiggled in an attempt to fit her body better between Alex and the hard granite, he told her to stay put. "It will get hot in here fast. In a minute, I can vent the top, but they'll probably fly back over. We need to hunker down a little while."

A hard shiver ran through her. "What if there's a snake hunkering with us?"

A deep chuckle rumbled up from his chest. "Trust you to think of that with a predator drone overhead and two SUVs full of hired guns canvassing the area."

To her alarm, a completely unexpected sob escaped her. The blanket rustled as she slid her hand over her mouth.

"Kate. What is it?"

"I'm so tired of running and hiding. I know, I know, you don't have to say it." Her voice thinned as she strangled on her own guilt. "This latest round of terror is my fault. I'm an idiot."

"I wasn't going to say that." His voice dipped to that murmur that warmed her insides. "You just need to learn where to place your trust."

Kate felt his arm scoop under her and allowed him to turn her cheek onto his chest. No, not allowed. *Welcomed.* She let the hot tears seep from under her eyelids as Alex rubbed a hand over her back. She felt so ridiculously happy to have him hold her that she almost forgot drones, dogs, and snakes.

"You're right." After a long moment of silence except for the rustling of the Mylar and their shallow breathing, she admitted the rest. "But I do trust you."

Her hope for a reciprocal statement expired with Alex's short admission. "Her name was Shayna."

"Who?"

"The female recruit. None of us wanted her in our company. We didn't want the drama, the hype, the challenges, of training with a woman. We didn't think she'd make it. But something had made her tough ... something in her past she'd never talk about. She just kept hanging on. Eventually, she got to be like our bratty little sister. There were still some jerks who would've pressed their advances on her, so as specialist team leader, I made sure none of them got inappropriate."

Kate's heart warmed that he'd chosen to share this with her, even if it was only because he knew it would distract her, calm her down. "Of course you did." She spread her palm on his chest as if he was hers to touch and be proud of, and waited. His rib cage rose with a deep breath. No doubt he struggled as she did to get enough air under the hot space blanket.

"We patrolled the area outside Kabul in Wardak Province and trained the Afghan National Police in their duties. By 2012, Taliban insurgents took shots at our guys daily. They intimidated the local shopkeepers into shutting down the markets and frightened the girls into staying home from school. Roadside explosives became common. Explosives very like the one that went off at the Fox."

Kate nodded. Then she swallowed as his fingers twined in her hair. The gesture almost seemed to comfort him. He continued, his voice steady again.

"One day we were traveling from base to the city in two Mine Resistant Ambush Protected Vehicles. Shayna was in the one behind mine. It ran over an IED that exploded."

Her chest tightened even more. "Oh, Alex." She braced herself for what might come next.

"My sergeant thought everyone in the vehicle was killed, but I got on the radio, and Shayna answered. She sounded bad. She said the others were dead and she was 'done for,' bleeding out fast. When she described her wound, and the sergeant took into account the small arms and rocket-propelled grenade fire they'd opened up into the ravine, he ordered us back to base. She wasn't answering anymore, but I couldn't do it. I couldn't leave her."

"The Warrior Ethos," Kate whispered. "You went back for her."

"Yeah. One of my buddies went with me to provide cover. When we reached Shayna, she was barely alive. I carried her out, but Sam … he didn't make it."

She reached for his hand and squeezed. "I'm so sorry, Alex. Shayna? Did she?"

"She died while I was carrying her to our vehicle." His voice broke, and the hum of the returning drone swelled in the silence. Alex tucked the blanket tighter.

She hardly paid attention. At the moment, the drone felt like an annoying distraction rather than the threat it was. Kate pressed on with her questioning. "And you left the army after that?"

"My tour ended the next month, and I was politely asked to not sign up again."

"I see. So rather than give you a medal for bravery, they kicked you out. Nice. But Alex … you do know you didn't do anything wrong, don't you?"

"Doesn't matter. My decision cost Sam his life. How could they explain to his family that my irrational insistence on saving a female soldier who could not be saved made their son die?"

"Compassion is not something to be ashamed of, Alex. You made the best decision you could under the circumstances. The right one, I believe. So did Sam." She paused for another deep breath. "Shayna knew the risks when she signed up. Again, so did Sam."

Alex made a grunting sound that acknowledged her efforts but fell short of indicating agreement.

She tightened her fingers over his. Despite the fact that she could hardly breathe, there was something she had to know. "Did you ... have feelings for her?"

"Romantic ones?" He grunted again. "No. But that doesn't change the fact that my emotions and my protective instincts overshadowed my professional judgment."

"Is that why you didn't want your partner on this TV show to be a woman?"

"Partly. The other part I already told you."

Kate felt her cheeks heat even more. Alex loosed his hand from hers to trace the line of her chin. Distracted by the physical and emotional closeness, she forgot to be afraid of the drone or the people flying it who must be somewhere near this part of the lake.

"I'm glad it wasn't just that you thought I'd be a helpless mess," Kate said, "although I admit I have been."

"You've been brave and flexible and exasperating and funny ... and far more than I ever expected." His voice turned gravelly at the end.

"Thanks. And you've been ... exactly opposite of what I expected. In a good way." She gave a soft laugh.

"The *last* thing I expected was for you to respond like you did about Shayna."

"Really? You thought I'd judge you?"

"It was the biggest mistake of my life. It ended my career ... and a man's life."

"I believe in your decision, Alex." Kate whispered the sweet truth. "I believe in you."

His silence told her that her gift of grace had hit the mark. He brushed her hair back where it stuck to her neck. "Cade was right. Between what happened with Shayna and my wonderful past with my dad, I've learned it's easier to keep people at arm's length. It's not been that hard. Girlfriends couldn't handle me being in the military, and since I got back to Atlanta, I work. I keep to myself. I volunteer to stay busy. Then they threw me together with you for this show. And you just seem to keep … creeping closer."

His words caused the memory of the conversation Kate had overheard at the campfire to leap back into her mind. Indignation fired her response. "I'm not creeping. You made it perfectly clear you don't want a commitment, and I still intend to honor that."

"Shh." Alex put a finger over her lips.

She brushed his hand away. "Stop shushing me. Why are you always doing that?"

"Right now, because I want to take back what I said. What you heard."

She tilted her head up. "You do?"

"I have this stupid habit of arguing even when I know I'm beat, and that's what I was doing with Cade. What you heard was a dying man's last gasp, my own efforts to convince myself I could go back to regular life after this is over. But it's not true."

"It's not?" Her heart stuttered, then hammered out a ridiculous rhythm.

"Definitely not. Because no matter what I did, I'd never be able to forget this feisty redhead who's not a redhead—"

Afraid to follow him on this thread of hope, Kate interrupted. "What about when you told me we had nothing in common, that we bonded because of the stressful circumstances?"

He fell silent a moment. "That was my biggest fear … that we can't fairly judge what's between us against this insane backdrop. But if we can make it through this, working together, still wanting to be with each other, maybe we can make it through anything."

When his arm tightened, drawing her closer and higher, her head on his shoulder, she allowed hope to blossom. "Maybe shared, basic beliefs are most important."

"And the differences complement. Like being two halves of a whole."

That did it. She leaned up and, finding his jaw with her fingers, kissed him.

Chapter Seventeen

On the Run Day 7
7:15 p.m.

The world looked different when Alex folded back the Mylar blanket a few minutes later. There was no sound of the drone, but a light rain had started to fall from the heavy sky. Alex expected Kate to complain about hiking in the drizzle, but she didn't seem to notice. She fixed her ponytail, cheeks bright.

"We better get going." He folded the Mylar and stuffed it into his pack. "The Johnsons won't have anticipated the delay from the drone."

Kate took a sip of water and nodded. When he held out his hand, she allowed him to help her up. He gave a tug that anchored her against his chest, then lowered his lips to hers. He loved how soft and yielding she felt against him. He wanted to say he loved her, but he couldn't until they were out of danger. Until they'd tested their connection in normal life. Even separation. He settled for looking into her eyes, making her a promise. "We're going to get out of this."

She nodded again.

Working together, no longer at odds, they'd make it to the highway. From there, they'd figure out the next steps.

Alex shouldered his pack, then turned to help Kate with hers. "Follow me. I'll try to take the clearest way without leaving an obvious trail, in case someone is following."

That trail sometimes wound through the woods where the underbrush remained clear and the creek descended into a gulley, at other times traced only a step or two from the water. Without complaint, Kate stayed close behind him. But as the terrain grew more rugged, her breathing shortened. As they climbed away from the lake, the stream plummeted over fallen logs and sections of rocky shoals, bubbling like a mountain brook. The cloud cover made visibility difficult, and as darkness advanced, Alex took increasingly to the open route of the creek bed.

"Be careful." He spoke over his shoulder after leaping onto a tilted rock. "Step on the moss when you can. The rain's making the rocks slick."

He'd barely issued the warning when he heard Kate make the jump behind him, then cry out, accompanied by the sound of gravel sliding. He whipped around to find her sprawled on the ground, clutching her left leg.

"Kate!" He hurried back and knelt beside her.

"Don't say it." She moaned, rocking back and forth. "Don't say 'I told you so.'"

"I won't. Anyway, you just did. What happened, you twisted your ankle?"

"*And* cut it on that broken branch."

Alex pried Kate's hand away to inspect the puncture wound that already oozed blood down to her heel. He did everything he could to keep his face calm, to not let on that this could be a serious game-changer. "I don't think it's terribly deep, but we've got to get this bandaged. Can you lean on me to get to that rock over there?" Sliding Kate's backpack off her shoulders, he nodded toward a boulder overlooking a quiet pool that jutted out from the creek.

"Yes." She placed her arm around his neck and hobbled with him. At least the trees broke the light rain. As he fetched his first aid kit, she extended her leg. But when she tried to turn it to expose the calf, she whimpered in pain.

Alex ripped open an antiseptic wipe. "Ankle's swelling."

Kate bit her lip as he tended the cut as gently as possible, applying ointment, then a thick gauze pad and adhesive tape.

"Can you stand?"

She tried but collapsed back onto the rock, shaking her head. He remained kneeling, palpitating her ankle with a light touch. Leaving her was the last thing he wanted to do. But not knowing how far they remained from the road or how steep the terrain would become, it made the most sense to come back for her. He surveyed the line of boulders leading into a cleft in the bank. Standing up, he pushed aside foliage to inspect the rock overhang, almost like a small cave.

"Dry. Unoccupied," he said. "And big enough for a person to sit inside."

Horror deepened her voice as she followed his thought pattern. "Oh no. You are not leaving me here."

He kept his voice even. "That's a bad sprain, Kate. I could make it to the road a lot faster on my own and be back with help by dark."

"What if help isn't there?" Not bothering to push the stray hair from her eyes, she gazed up at him, unblinking.

Alex's middle clenched. Here was the moment he'd tried to avoid by keeping his emotions at bay. And he still had to use logic if they were going to make it out of this forest alive. "Emma will have called the police."

"You are not leaving me alone in a dark forest with snakes and bears and crazed gunmen on the loose."

"I'd leave you the Beretta." Alex patted the holster on his hip. "Remember, I showed you how to load and fire it in the Lenox house." He hoped she'd been paying attention.

"I'm going with you. Just try to stop me." Panic made her voice wobble as much as her body as she hoisted herself to one foot and started to hop over to her pack.

She was being unreasonable. "There's no way you can carry that."

"Then I'll leave it. Find me a big stick to lean on."

He rushed over to steady her before she lost her balance. "Don't be stupid, Kate."

She turned her gaze on him and played her final card. "'I will never leave a fallen comrade.'"

All the breath rushed out of him in a sigh of defeat. If he hadn't left Shayna, he couldn't leave Kate. And she knew it.

After bracing her against a tree, he transferred a few essentials—a flashlight, LifeStraw drinker, fire starter, bandaging supplies, a few Powerbars, a map, and a burner phone—from his backpack to a smaller bag, then shoved their packs under the overhang. When he returned to Kate, he turned around backwards. "Get on. I'll take you to the top of that hill."

"And then what?" With a grunt, Kate gave the best hop she could muster and latched her arms around his neck.

Alex hoisted her up and, careful of her ankle, tugged her legs around his waist. He jerked his chin towards the rise. "I think the mill ruins may be up there."

"Should we really leave our packs?" She tightened her grip, breath from her question tickling his ear.

"Not like you give me much choice." Alex started forward, bending a bit to compensate for the increased load. "If those are the ruins up ahead, we're close enough that I can carry you out."

"If not?"

"If not, I'm bringing you back to the cave, and you'll wait there like I said."

Wisely, Kate refrained from argument. With his hands holding her legs in place, she tried to reach ahead to divert wily branches.

At the top, a wide shoals came into view. "A stone wall." She pointed a finger into the dim forest ahead. "And that's a foundation. This is it!"

"According to the map, the dirt road runs just beyond the mill. We should see the remains of a connecting drive nearby."

Past the ruins, ghostly in the twilight, a partial dam still created a deep pool at the head of the shoals. Thick branches overhung the placid water. Alex turned in the clearing until they spotted a patch of red Georgia clay. They followed the path they found to the intersection of a perpendicular, double-rutted lane.

Relief rolled through him like a powerful shot of adrenaline. "Yes! We're almost there. Should be about another mile to 306. Let's take a water break and call the number Emma gave us."

He allowed Kate to slide down his back until her foot touched the ground, then he helped her to a fallen log out of view of the dirt road. He inserted his LifeStraw into his drinker and handed it to her before taking a drink himself. When they finished, he blew into the mouthpiece to purge the water from the filter.

Extending her leg, Kate froze. "Um ... I may not have helped this cut by trying to hold onto you with my legs."

The wound had already bled through the wrapping. This time, Alex couldn't stop himself from snapping. "Kate! And this ankle is twice the size it was back at the cave. It needs ice ... and elevation. This is bad."

As he fumbled in his pocket for an extra piece of gauze, she wiped a tear away. "No way around it now. You're going to have to leave me in the woods."

Alex glanced up. "Hey. It's okay. I'm going to make this call. I'll tell them you need medical attention, and help will be here in no time."

Kate nodded and watched him get out the phone, but when he turned it on and held it up, he let out a growl. Stood up. Turned in a circle.

"Don't tell me. No reception." Dread deepened her tone. "Should've known."

"I have one bar. No dial tone. We'll have to climb up higher."

"What's that?" Kate's question quivered in the air, breathless and high-pitched. Before he could respond, she plopped onto the ground behind the tree.

Once again, her senses had proved sharper than his. The low hum of a large vehicle's engine coming their way prompted Alex to dart for cover beside her. Kate seized a nearby branch with the dried leaves still attached and pulled it over both of them.

If she hadn't been alert ...

Placing a hand on his chest, Kate asked in a low voice, "Can you see?"

"Yes. Shh."

As she eased her hurt leg away from him, he palmed the Beretta.

With the swishing of underbrush, the vehicle passed slowly, as if its occupants scanned their surroundings on both sides.

"One black SUV," Alex whispered. When it kept going, Kate let out a sigh of relief. "Probably going to rendezvous with the other. They may turn around at the creek. We've got to go. Now." He tossed the branch to the side and holstered the pistol, then grabbed his bag.

"Okay. Where?" She struggled to get back on the log.

"I'm taking you back to that cliff."

Kate's silence acknowledged that he couldn't evade their pursuers fast enough while carrying her through the dense forest. He didn't bother to try to get her on his back again but scooped her up in horizontal position and darted back the way they came. His training made him sure-footed even in the dusk. Only keeping her swollen ankle from hitting trees slowed Alex down as he angled and maneuvered his way down the hill.

"With the hunters so close, how will you get to the highway?" She tightened her arms around his neck.

"I'm expecting them to search the mill ruins. I'll cut through the woods to skirt that area."

"You haven't gotten the call out yet. What if no one is at the road when you get there?"

He slowed down to cross damp, rocky ground near the cave. Small pebbles rolled beneath his boots. "I'll call as soon as I get reception. Best case, they're already there. Worst case, I should only have to wait a few minutes."

"But I won't know ... I won't know ..."

"Kate." Alex spoke her name to calm her as he ducked to enter the overhang. The scent of damp, growing things swirled around them, rich and loamy. Shoving their bags around with a boot, he settled her under the rock, then slid one of the packs under her ankle. He placed a gentle hand on her shin. "You *do* know."

A small sob escaped her lips as she looked around the dim crevice that barely concealed her. He squeezed her leg, prompting her to meet his eyes. "You know I'll come back for you. You know I can do this. And I know you can too. I realize I'm asking everything that's hard for you right now, leaving you in danger, feeling helpless and hurt, and in a tiny space, of all places. But will you trust me? Will you trust God?"

The tears bubbled over, and wrapping her arms around his neck, Kate leaned her forehead against his. She nodded, then sought the reassurance of his lips. He kissed her, firm and fast. Then he pressed the gun into her hand.

"No." Kate grabbed for him as he lunged away. "You can't go out there without your pistol."

"I can't leave you here without it either. Just be sure you don't shoot me when I come back. And Kate, I'm taking the burner phone. You have the other one. The number's written in my notebook. You have a flashlight, but only call if it's an emergency. We don't want to attract attention at the wrong moment."

She tried to scramble out of the opening in the rock. "Alex—"

He held out a hand toward her, and his voice almost failed. "Stop, Kate. Please, don't make this any harder. Stay quiet. Stay hidden. I'll call you when I'm close by."

Kate couldn't decide which to clutch, the phone or the pistol, so she laid both in her lap, but it terrified her to hold a loaded gun. She hadn't actually gotten to practice firing at the Lenox house. Alex had just showed her the basics. She'd never even been to a shooting range. Truth was, she was probably safer without the weapon, but Alex's chivalry wrapped around her like a warm blanket, his protective gesture more comforting than the gun.

She longed to call him, to make sure he'd contacted the Johnsons. But what if the phone rang when the SWAT guys came within hearing range? She couldn't endanger his life to calm her nerves. She had to trust.

The rain stopped, thick drops plopping right in front of her face from the rock orifice into the mud at her feet. An owl hooted from the coming darkness above her. The dripping trees faded to dim silhouettes. The creek rushed, swirling near her feet. Her leg ached, and her bandage oozed, soppy with liquid. A twig snapped nearby, and she stiffened. Could predators smell the blood? Fear crawled over her.

There's nothing I can do. She sat up straighter. *There is something I can do. I can pray.*

The notion felt stilted and unnatural, but reaching in her bag for a blanket and shrugging it around her shoulders from the front, she did just that.

Thirst pricked her throat, and Kate shifted, feeling around for the drinker. Of course it had fallen to the bottom of her knapsack. A voice of warning spoke in her head.

Be still.

What was that? Pausing, Kate strained both her eyes and ears to penetrate the dark night. The *schmucking* sound mud makes when disturbed and the roll of loose gravel told her something was out there. Holding her breath, Kate wrapped her fingers around the Beretta.

Seconds passed in silence. Finally, she eased out the breath she'd been holding. Must have been deer or raccoon passing by. She was about to resume her search for the drinker when a shaft of light flicked on. Her heart hammered. Slow and steady, Kate leaned in an attempt to see around the dangling underbrush. The flashlight illuminated the face of the man studying Alex's prints near the creek. Clayton. The gasp left her before she could stop it.

He swung the flashlight in her direction, and she ducked farther into the cave. "Alex? Kate? Is that you?" When only silence answered, he continued, circling on the bank, shining his light into the trees. "I just want to talk to you. See? I'm alone. Kate, I don't see your footprints. If you're there, I'm worried about you. Worried something happened. This is ridiculous. Let me take you out of this dark night and to the police."

As doubts rushed in, the innate but illogical desire to assure him she was safe ballooned inside her chest. What if the SWAT guys with him were part of his team of hired help, not the same ones who'd fired on them at the homeless shelter? What if they'd roared away from the gate at Peaceful Cove out of frustration and fear? But then ... why wouldn't the driver give his badge number to Emma? Kate bit her lip.

No. She would wait for Alex.

But Clayton was still talking, still coming closer. "Kate, please. I just want a little information. For us to come to an agreement. Then this can all be over, I promise."

Information? Agreement? That wasn't what he'd said on the phone.

He bent over, advancing on the inlet. He'd noticed the cave. As she attempted to flatten herself into the rock, the phone slid off her leg. Her lunge to catch it twisted her ankle, wrenching a gasp of pain from her lips as the cell hit the ground.

His tone changed from business-like to eager, concerned, and cajoling. "Kate? Sweetie? I know you're in there. Are you hurt?"

There was no use pretending. A few more steps and he'd see for himself that she was both injured and alone. Kate infused all the bravado she could muster into her tone. "Go away, Clayton. I have a gun."

"Where is Alex? Did he leave you? ... Figures."

"He would never leave me." Alex wouldn't, and neither would God. She had to believe that right now.

"Then why isn't he talking to me instead of you? Look, he's confused you, Kate. Due to his experiences in the military, he's not a stable man. Come out and we can talk." But Clayton's scan of his periphery told her he feared Alex remained nearby. He unholstered his own sidearm and laid it on the ground at his feet, taking a few steps back before sitting on a rock. "There. You see my intentions are honorable."

"Since when do you carry a gun?" Despite her effort to sound accusing, her voice quavered.

"Since maniacs hired by SurveyCorp have been hunting you."

"I'll take my chances. If you're telling me the truth, show me that by leaving."

Laying the flashlight on the boulder next to him so that it shone toward her crevice, Clayton placed his hands on his knees. "I'm not going anywhere."

God, what do I do?

The phone at her feet rang, jangling a breath of alarm out of her chest. She scrambled for it, snatched it up. Breathed into the receiver. "Alex?"

His voice, his blessed voice, hissed back. "Kate. I'm at the mill ruins."

Panic, desperation, and relief all bled into a cocktail so potent Kate's head spun. "Clayton is here. He's seen me. Come—"

Clayton jerked the phone out of her hand and threw it into the water, wrenching her out of the cave by her elbow. She hadn't even seen him coming. He dragged Kate to her feet, twisting her swollen ankle, and she cried out in pain.

"You stupid, dramatic redhead!" He spat the accusation at her, pulling her arm. "You were always so stubborn. Now you're coming with me."

Kate hopped behind him but fell when her weight shifted to her left leg. Hands contacting small rocks and mud, she let out a sob.

"What's the matter with you? Get up!"

Before he could reach down to pull her again, she heard the same sound she had at the homeless shelter, and something skidded into the water next to her. A bullet.

Clayton whirled and shouted toward the surrounding bank. "NO! I told you not to hurt her!"

A faint *thump* sounded, followed by a *whoosh*. He flung himself over the top of her, and it was only when he kept falling and his full weight rested on her that she realized the next bullet had found a mark. Screams of terror rent her throat. Instinct told her to shove Clayton off, but another, still logical part knew that if she did, the next bullet would find her.

"Forsyth County Sheriff's Office." A man's voice bellowed through the darkness. "Lay down your weapon!"

Search lights illuminated the forest, and a tussle of some sort came from the trees that loomed over the creek. Then a man holding another bright light ran to the bank and fixed her location in his beam.

"She's here! Are you all right, ma'am?"

Kate managed a nod.

"She's unharmed. Don't move, ma'am."

She couldn't if she wanted to. Clayton's weight pinned her to the ground. His head slumped against her shoulder, and something hot and wet seeped into her shirt. Ragged weeping jerked her body as she tried to reposition his head. His blond hair smelled of familiar, spicy shampoo. As Kate cupped his face, his blue eyes fixed on her, pupils dilated. Twin talons of betrayal and regret clawed her chest.

"I'm ... sorry. Wanted to ... convince you. I didn't think he would hurt you."

"Who, Clayton?" She sensed somehow that he meant someone besides the shooter on the bank. "Who?"

"Dad."

Shock silenced her as a deputy retrieved Clayton's sidearm, then pulled him off her. When the officer reached for his handcuffs, she stirred and protested. "That's not necessary. This man needs medical attention."

A wonderfully familiar voice spoke from somewhere above. Not God, but close enough for the moment. "So does she."

Kate tried to pull herself to a sitting position as a dark shape scrambled down the bank. She held out her arms. Alex drew her close, and she buried her face against his chest and let the tears run down her cheeks.

Chapter Eighteen

Day 8
9:20 a.m.

By the time Alex left the holding room of the Forsyth County Sheriff's Office, no amount of thick, black, police-brewed coffee could have retained his clarity. The caffeine he'd consumed in the last ten hours did, however, fire his impatience to see Kate.

Alex had carried her out of the forest. She'd laid her head on his shoulder and closed her eyes. Sensing her trust, he'd been loath to transfer her to the businesslike paramedics who met them on the highway. Due to the puncture wound, they'd insisted on taking Kate to the emergency room, but he rode in the front of the ambulance.

At the hospital, it seemed to take forever for the X-ray and stitches to be ordered. Every time the nurses left the room, Alex switched off the bright light and leaned his head next to hers, trying to bolster Kate's strength with his silent presence.

Finally, it was on to the sheriff's office. He expected the officers to take their initial statement together, but to his dismay, they'd escorted them to different holding rooms. Thankfully, he was told that Lance had arrived and been allowed to join his sister.

Maybe by now Lance had persuaded the officers to allow Kate a rest. Many more hours of interviews lay ahead, including officers from other counties and the GBI, but Alex wanted to see her before he left. He needed to tell her why he couldn't go home with her.

When he approached the waiting room, relief spiraled through him that Kate stood there, leaning on her crutches. Lance and a ruffle-headed Cade shook hands as she introduced them, then, back facing Alex's approach, Lance addressed his sister.

"My understanding was that Alex would go to the safe house the GBI arranged. The only reason you're not going there is because I can take care of you."

"And I can take care of myself." Alex walked through the door and locked arms with Cade in greeting. "Hey, man. Thank you for coming and waiting. I thought maybe you could suggest a place close to Peaceful Cove. I've got some things to figure out, and if Emma's not opposed, I'd like to talk to you guys some more."

"Emma's on board, Alex. Ever since we got your call, she's been on the phone arranging other places for the two ladies we had. She wants you to come back with me." Cade patted his shoulder and flashed a brief smile. "You can stay with us until you're called to Atlanta."

"That would be great."

Alex turned to Kate, steeling himself to face the hurt in her eyes. For the past week, he'd moved them around like chess pieces evading the hunters, always certain of himself, but now he didn't know his next move ... and he didn't know how to tell her that.

She lifted her chin. "I guess I'll see you then. Whenever *then* is. In Atlanta."

Recognizing her defensive move, Alex didn't try to hide his sadness and regret. He glanced at Cade and Lance. "Guys, would you mind giving me a few minutes with Kate?"

"Sure." Cade responded quickly. "We'll go get the cars and pull up front. Lance?" He prompted Kate's brother, who stood frowning at Alex. Moving slow and glancing back over his shoulder several times, Lance followed Cade to the main entrance.

"Sit down a minute. Your ankle must be throbbing." Alex gestured to a pair of chairs in the corner of the almost-vacant room.

Kate allowed him to help her and position her crutches against the wall, but she folded her hands in her lap and wouldn't meet his gaze. She blinked away the moisture glinting in her eyes.

His heart ached that in order to figure out his next step, he had to cause her pain. "Kate, look at me."

She gave her head a brisk shake. She'd probably have stalked out of there if her ankle wasn't the size of a small watermelon.

Alex reached for her hand, and when he spoke, his voice was so thick that she glanced up in surprise. "I'm not leaving you." His throat worked as he fought for control, and now he was the one who wouldn't look at her. "I don't expect it will take them long to call us to Atlanta, but I have to decide some major things about what comes after that, and I can't do that if I'm with you."

"Why not?"

He sought her gaze. "Because when I'm with you, you're all I think about."

She pressed a hand over her mouth.

"I think I'm falling in love with you, Kate, but we're tired, we're traumatized, we're emotional. And we have big decisions ahead. I need to be able to think and pray. Cade can help me with that—"

"Wait." Her fingers fluttered to the camo-patterned sleeve of his green jacket. "What did you say? At the beginning of that spill?"

He took that hand too. "I said I think I'm falling in love with you."

Despite the stares of the man sitting across the room who looked like a drug dealer and the hefty female officer on duty behind the glassed-in desk, Kate reached for him.

Alex wrapped his arms around her and continued, whispering into her muddy-brown hair. "I promise you, this is not the last time you'll see me. We have a lot to talk about, but right now, neither one of us has perspective or clarity."

"There's so much I don't understand about what happened."

"You were hurt, betrayed." He rubbed a thumb along her temple. "We don't even know to what extent. The investigation will give us answers, but we'll need to take time to process all this, and we need to do that with people who love and support us."

"You're right." When Kate drew back, fresh strength glowed on her face. "And not just our friends or families, but God. I've also got to make decisions differently than I have in the past. Although ..." A faint smile flitted across her face. "I already have an idea about some of the things God wants in my future."

"What do you mean?"

"Come closer, and I'll tell you."

When he leaned in, Kate sealed his lips with hers.

Chapter Nineteen

Day 28
3:10 p.m.

"It's hard to believe this is where it all started." Kate snapped a lid onto her café mocha and swept a hand to encompass the long, butcher block bar of Heavenly Grounds. "At least, the real danger."

Waiting with her streusel muffin in one hand and her light roast in the other, Amber agreed. "I'll never forget the moment that car almost hit you. I knew you were in serious trouble and that you'd been trying to give me something at the press conference. That was when I started asking questions. But until the GBI interviewed key employees and I got a copy of what was on the flash drive, no one was talking."

"And now, you get the scoop of the decade." She nodded to the folded *AJC* her friend had stuck in Kate's leather bag. "I can't wait to read the article."

Amber snorted. "Not like you don't know everything in it."

"Well, I'm still going to savor every word because you wrote it, and now the public knows the full truth."

Amber disagreed as they settled at a table near the window. "Not the full truth." Behind her, a tween girl swung her legs from a stool as she sipped a blended frozen drink with a mound of whipped cream on top. Amber rolled her eyes. "Where's her mom? Shouldn't she be in school? Anyway, as I was saying, my inboxes have been blowing up all day with people wanting to know what's next for you and Alex."

Which was one of the reasons she was meeting Amber here today. Pushing down a yearning sense of regret, Kate opened the newspaper on the surface in front of her. "Trust people to demand the soap opera romance angle when they should be focusing on the arrest of the mayor."

"Oh, believe me, there's plenty of vitriol about the sinister plot to establish a surveillance city, but people fell in love with you and Alex when they watched you on TV, Kate. You're the heroes of this horrible story. The public was incensed that *Traces* refused to hand out any prize money after all you went through. With your lives in danger, it's not as though you had a choice about ditching the cameras."

"Well, no one actually made it twenty days." Kate ran a finger along the crease that halved the front page.

"Yes, but you would have, had someone not been trying to kill you."

"That's not important. All the stuff that came out during the investigation is. I'm sorry Alex won't return your calls. He barely stays in touch with me right now. He's interviewing this week with the Albany Police Department and trying to work things out with his parents. He says they have appointments every day with financial advisors, doctors, and counselors … even his parents' pastor. It's personal stuff he wouldn't want in the paper. I'll try to give you something about where I'm at for a sidebar follow-up on my story, and maybe that will satisfy, but right now, I want to read this."

"Of course." Amber sat back and nibbled her muffin, giving Kate a chance to read out loud.

"'GBI officials and detectives of the Atlanta Police Department arrested Atlanta Mayor Gerald Barnes and key members of his staff this Monday, May twenty-eighth, at his Trinity Avenue office. The arrest warrants were issued after computer and phone evidence revealed that Barnes conspired with SurveyCorp President Justin Sandler and certain directors of the surveillance manufacturer to detonate the bomb that exploded outside the Fox Theatre last December, killing a father and two children. Employees of then-mayoral candidate Barnes and President Sandler, with their approval, allegedly arranged for an Islamic extremist cell to plant the IED and take credit for the attack. They counted on the resulting backlash to propel Barnes into office and generate public support for installation of The Eye Above Atlanta, the thirteen-lens, military-derived camera now surveilling the city from atop the BankCorp-SurveyCorp building.'"

Mumbling phrases aloud here and there, she skimmed the next part that summarized how her participation in *Traces* brought the crimes to light. She sat back and took a deep breath. "This is the biggest story to break in Atlanta since Sherman. What will this do for your career?"

Amber smiled. "What it's done for yours. I'm being offered a promotion."

"Wow. Congratulations!" Even though Kate was not nearly as excited about her own advancement as she was about her friend's, at least some good could come of this tragedy.

Her friend shrugged a shoulder. "Some always rise when others fall. Keep reading. You'll like the next part."

Clearing her throat, she attempted to broadcast her voice over the slurping behind Amber as the teeny bopper sucked the whipping from the bottom of her cup. "'Alton Clark, SurveyCorp vice president of technology development, who oversaw the civilian adaption of The Eye and his assistant, Kendra Reed, director of technology information, played key roles in the liaison between the mayor's office and the technology mogul.'" Kate paused, distracted by the motion of the now-frappe-less girl tossing expresso beans into her mouth.

Amber widened her eyes at Kate. "She's gonna be wired when her mom picks her up. Exactly what the woman will deserve. Ignore her. Keep going."

"'Reed worked with the company's public relations department to develop marketing materials and strategies. Officers took both Clark and Reed into custody with simultaneous Monday arrests. SurveyCorp's board of directors also relieved Vice President of Public Relations Helen O'Ruark of her position. Evidence disclosed that O'Ruark publicized the joint response of the mayor-elect and her company to the bombing without reporting the suspicious circumstances surrounding the incident. Kate Carson, SurveyCorp's former external communications manager tapped by her employer to participate in the *Traces* reality TV show, now fills O'Ruark's position.'" Kate paused and looked up. "Temporarily."

"You don't think Helen will get her job back, do you?"

"No. I think she'll retire and spend the rest of her days defending her innocence. And I truly think she didn't know, but as I almost did, she made the decision to look the other way in order to maintain her job."

"At least your efforts to shine the light led to some reward … the new position. I just can't believe you're not more excited about that. I mean, I know it pales in comparison to everything terrible that's happened, but Kate, it's what you've worked for this whole time." Amber's brown hair swung over her cheek as she shook her head in emphasis.

Kate sighed and tucked a strand of her own hair, now red again and satisfyingly longer, behind her ear. She glanced down at her silk blouse and light-gray, tailored suit, the name brand pumps on her feet … and felt empty. How did she explain that to Amber?

"Are you really not going to stay in the job?"

"I want to help reorganize the department. I owe SurveyCorp that much. Now that there's talk of shutting down The Eye, I hope to stay until they're back on their feet again, focusing on their core products." Kate paused to take a sip of her café mocha. Its smooth richness soothed her empty stomach.

"But?" Amber prompted her.

"But I hope to ease back into my writing. Not just press releases and brochures, but books. I don't know how yet, but when I was on the run, things got pretty hairy a couple of times." She shook her head. "That stress made me start to question some things. I think I'm meant to use my writing in a deeper way."

"Okay …"

The uncertain way Amber's voice trailed off assured Kate she didn't fully get it. That was all right.

Amber shifted the conversation back to ground she could stand on. "I know what happened with Clayton's going to take some time to get over. The next part talks about him." She turned the paper with a finger, skimming it with her gaze. "You may not want to read it. The database of surveillance targets was his idea."

Kate mumbled into her coffee. "I still can't believe I was dating the guy but had no idea he hated so many groups of people."

"You can't blame yourself. That's not the kind of thing people talk about."

"If you love someone, you do. You have to share the same core beliefs."

Amber nodded, giving her a sympathetic smile that showed she realized Kate referred to Alex. "At least Clayton didn't plan the bombing."

"Yet when he learned about it afterwards, he didn't say anything."

"True, and he told his father he suspected you got something off his computer. That's when Gerald hired the hit men. Clayton's statements to the police support what he told you at his arrest, that he thought he could convince you SurveyCorp alone was at fault."

"And use my evidence against them to convince the police." Kate twisted her mouth to one side. "He didn't think his father would actually try to take me out."

"Gerald Barnes has a whole heap of charges mounting against him. I hope you know that your testimony will be required at a long and painful trial quite some time in the future. This isn't going to be a book you can close easily."

She ducked her head. "I know." *If Alex is by my side, I can do it.* She corrected herself. *No, with God by my side, I can do it.* She just hoped God knew Alex's presence would help too.

"Maybe this is the book you can write."

"Maybe." That wasn't the first time someone had said that. Hmm. Wasn't confirmation supposed to come in threes?

Kate returned to the thought that had comforted her many a restless night where Clayton was concerned. "At least Clayton's sentence shouldn't be as harsh as his father's. I know I saw humanity in him, Amber. I mean, he flung himself on top of me to save me."

"Yes, I'm glad he's recovering from that. I've always thought he's spent his whole life under the thumb of a very controlling father."

"I still have hope that he'll come out of this ordeal a changed man."

Amber nodded as she started digging in her bag. "Gerald, however, will never see the light of day again except from a prison exercise yard." She placed a recorder on the table between them, turning all business. "Now, what juicy statement can you give me for a follow-up story on you and Alex? Be generous, please. I have to deliver something to my starving readership."

The anticipatory grin Amber fixed on Kate above the fingers she tapped together made Kate laugh, but her voice broke in emotion she tried to cover with a cough. She ducked her head.

"Oh, Kate. That bad?" Pushing the recorder aside, Amber reached to pat her hand.

"He never even worked out a notice at SurveyCorp, although they offered him a generous raise to stay." And although she still stupidly looked for him every day behind the front desk. Kate pressed her hand to her stomach to quell the ache. "Who can blame him? No one wants to work for a company that helped arrange a bombing to promote its products. I don't know if SurveyCorp will even survive."

"Except that they have a monopoly on the country's surveillance technology. And *you* stayed."

"For a while. With the bad seeds tossed out, I believe in paying them back for the help they gave me when I needed it. But Alex didn't have that motivation." She shook her head and slid the sleeve on her coffee cup up and down. "His primary loyalty now is to his family."

Amber's skepticism showed on her softly rounded face. "Well, what about you? If he ever wants the chance to make you part of that family, he'd be smart not to disappear at such a crucial time, don't you think?"

Kate pulled her hand back, dropping it into her lap. "I don't know. I miss him so much it feels like someone carved out a chunk of me, but I have no idea how this can work between Albany and Atlanta."

Pressing her lips together in a prim line, her friend checked her phone. "Well, maybe he can help us with that. Five minutes ago, he said he was five minutes out."

"What?" Kate jerked her head up as her heartbeat stuttered. "He's here? In Atlanta?"

"Actually …" Amber looked out the window toward the busy street. "He's at the door."

A tall man in black pants and a button-down shirt strolled into the coffee shop. Kate stood, although her legs didn't feel as though they would hold her. Clean-shaven, dark hair neatly trimmed, Alex looked their way, and the smile that lit his face made her heart race again.

"This is … an ambush!"

"Yep." Amber practically cackled in delight.

Kate stood frozen until Alex walked over and reached for her. She put her arms around his neck and closed her eyes, trying to block out the busy shop and the staring tween at the counter until she could absorb the reality of his presence.

"Surprised?" he whispered against her ear.

She nodded.

Drawing back, he trailed his fingers through her hair in that way she remembered. He looked as though he wanted to kiss her, but with Amber gazing at them, smile as wide as the Chattahoochee River, he just said, "You look amazing," and pulled a chair over. As he placed it right next to hers, they both sank down, staring at each other.

Kate finally got out her question. "What are you doing here?"

"Well, of course he's responding to a star reporter's interview summons." Crossing her legs, Amber giggled.

Alex kept his eyes fixed on Kate. "Actually, I can't answer her questions until you answer mine."

A rush of adrenaline sent fire through her veins, but Amber snatched up her phone. "Ooh! This is gonna be good. Can I record this? Please? Whatever happens next will go viral two seconds after I post it, and it will be so much better than whatever I could write up."

"No recording." Alex pushed her hand down.

"What questions do you have?" Kate asked in a breathless voice.

He twisted his mouth into a thoughtful moue. "Mm, first big one is, do you miss me like I miss you?"

"I don't know." She glanced at Amber, willing her to silence. "How bad do you miss me?"

He sat forward so that his words would only sound like a murmur to Amber, but the steady gaze of his brown, lash-studded eyes underlined every one of them to Kate. "Like every morning I wake up, the day seems never-ending because you're not there. Like every time I think of something I want to tell you, it's not the same to text it. Like I'm missing my best friend, the only person I can talk to."

"Yes, I miss you like that. Is there more?"

He grinned at her whispered question. "More about how I miss you? Oh yeah."

She laughed, trying not to sound giddy. "More you need to ask me."

"Yes." Alex sat back a little as he reached for her hand, twining her fingers through his. "Second question is, how do you feel about South Georgia?"

"I think I'd need to do more than drive through to form an opinion."

"You know, I found the same thing ... about memories. Seems different now that I'm not seventeen anymore. The gnats are a pain, granted, but the cicadas, they can kinda put you to sleep at night. And the sunsets over the fields can be amazing. Especially if you have someone to share them with."

"Uh-huh." Kate nodded.

Biting her lip, Amber started scribbling on a notepad.

Alex continued, covering their joined hands with his other hand. "Following my training, I'll start part-time at the Albany Police Department. It will work into full-time in a month or two, after I get some things squared away with Mom and Dad. We've got a lot of decisions to make, but I'd like you to be part of them."

She blinked. "What do you mean? How can I be? I'm kind of tied up here for a while." Although she refrained from telling him that if he asked her to escape with him right this minute, she'd probably knock her chair over in her haste to exit.

"I know. But there's this studio apartment over the garage at the farm. Seems like a good writer's retreat." He winked and teased her knuckles with the tip of his index finger. "Maybe you'd want to come check it out this weekend, let me show you around, introduce you to my parents?"

"This weekend?" Kate placed her free hand over her heart.

"And every weekend you want to after that, if you like it?"

Did he actually phrase that like a question? Didn't he know she'd love it because he was there? But … "What if I like it, but they don't like me?"

"They can't wait to meet you. I think they're crediting half Jesus, half you, with the salvation of their son."

"Then, yes." The laugh of joy Kate no longer needed to repress bubbled out. "I'll drive down Friday night."

In response, a grin blazed across his features. "I love you, Kate."

He didn't give her a second to process his stunning revelation but swooped in to seal her lips with a kiss. Sliding a hand into the hair at the back of his neck, she kissed him back so well that he knew her answer before she spoke it.

"I love you, too, Alex."

He turned to smile at Amber, who sat watching their entire declaration with her mouth agape. Alex chuckled. "So there you have it, Miss Lassiter. For the record. She's coming to Albany."

"That's it? That's all I get for my romantic follow-up article?"

The girl behind Amber slid off her stool, tossing her French braid over her slender shoulder. Leaving her empty cup on the counter, she turned to grin at Kate and Alex. "Congratulations, guys. I'm happy for you. But I have to say, for being supposed experts in evading surveillance, you kinda stink. And you, star reporter …" Holding up her phone with a smug smile, she pressed a button that replayed the kiss Kate had just shared with Alex, now posted to her social media account. "You got scooped."

Kate's jaw dropped, but her euphoria was too strong right then for indignation to even stir. She did, however, feel bad for her friend. As the tween sashayed to the door, Amber stared after her and spluttered.

"My—my story …"

Kate leaned forward, placed a hand on Amber's arm, and whispered in her ear. "Don't worry about it. If this works out, my maid of honor will get the wedding exclusive."

Amber turned back to her with her eyes and lips rounding.

Kate glanced at Alex. Had he heard? As he had during the reality show, would he think she presumed too much, too fast?

Her anxiety was laid to rest with a grin and a wink.

Alex tilted his dark head toward Amber. "How 'bout you come on down this weekend with Kate? Do a little write-up on what my life is like now—and what it might be like for Kate in the future?"

"Really? That would be great. Beyond great. I mean, if that's okay with Kate."

Kate squeezed her hand. "Sure. I'd love to share my next adventure with my best friend. Who knows, maybe you'll even meet someone yourself." As Amber raised her eyebrows, digesting that possibility with a smile, Kate reached her arm around Alex's shoulders, nestling into his warmth and security. "Seems to me, these South Georgia boys are keepers."

Author's Note

D id you find the idea of The Eye farfetched? Think again.
As a writer, I look for the unique and the little-known—but the truthful or realistic—to inspire settings and plots. The idea for *Traces* began with a reality TV show that ran only one season in the U.S. (2017), but it captured my attention because I recognized many of the filming locations here in Georgia. The U.S. version of *Hunted* was an offshoot of the original, ongoing British version. In both shows, contestants seek to invade skilled investigators for a set amount of time in a set area in order to win a cash prize. The U.S. investigators included intelligence analysts, cyber analysts, a psychologist, and former employees of the U.S. Marshals, Department of Homeland Security, U.S. Army Special Forces, U.S. Secret Service, FBI, U.S. Army Rangers, SWAT, and police detectives. You can envision the challenge!

The second piece of *Traces* was The Eye, technology that may seem futuristic but for all intents and purposes already exists. Constant Hawk was developed in the early 2000s at Lawrence Livermore National Laboratory. The wide-area motion imagery (WAMI) system weighed around 1500 pounds and was flown on manned aircraft in Iraq and Afghanistan.

The technology from Constant Hawk has continued to evolve. Virginia-based Logos Technologies adapted the technology to a 150-pound version named Kestrel which was used in 2012 at the Arizona-Mexican border and a forty-pound version named Simera that omits infrared night-vision capabilities of military models. Brazilian officials mounted four Simera on weather balloons and small blimps to surveille the 2016 Rio Olympic Games. Thirteen full-motion cameras capable of zoom captured real-time footage with sixty times the resolution of high definition at three frames per second.

From these examples of existing WAMI systems, it's not hard to picture one being installed on a skyscraper. That type of surveillance makes some feel secure, but for others, it would represent a total loss of freedom. A perfect and unique setting for a suspense novel.

I hope you've enjoyed *Traces*. I greatly appreciate online reviews. They let my publisher know I should be published again! And I'd love to connect with you on social media, BookBub, and via monthly author e-mail. Learn more at https://deniseweimerbooks.webs.com